Danger at Tapestry Court

by Amy Barkman

Danger at Tapestry Court

Copyright © 2016

Published by Voice of Joy Publications

Cover design by Virginia Smith

ISBN: 978-0998352046

Dedication and Thank You

This book is dedicated, first of all to Jesus Christ, who gave me His own love for emotional healing and fighting evil in any way possible. Then to Ginny Smith, without whom I would never have gotten where I am as an author, to Betsy Banks who loved the first one so much that she encouraged me to write this one, and to Jacque Lea, my friend since 1953 and prayer partner since we got enough sense to pray. And last but not least to all who love cozy mysteries, Christian fiction, and Tapestry Court.

One of those is a special friend Gail Louis who proof-read both of the Tapestry Court books and said "*Danger* is a really delightful sequel to *Murder*. Not only is it a well-written mystery with plenty of suspense to keep you on your toes but it also gives the reader a message to use in our daily living. I am so proud that in a world that seems to be afraid to refer to God and speak of prayer, my friend is writing books with characters who believe in God and give Him a place of honor in their lives. I can hardly wait for the third book in the Tapestry Court series."

Tapestry Court
drawn by Chuck Tate

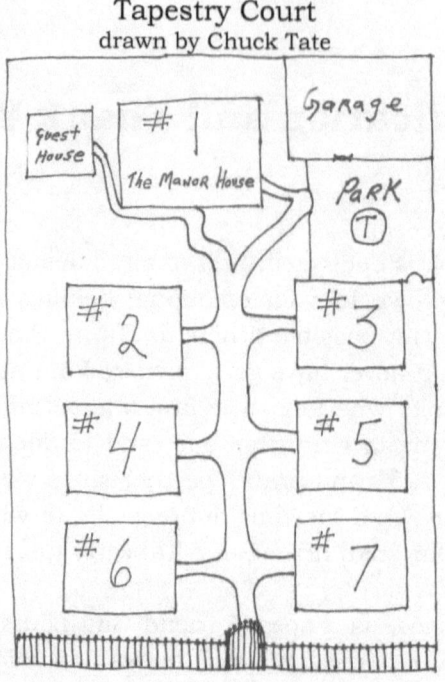

Number 1. The Manor House, former home of Colonel Guy Tapestry, founder of Tapestry Industries, is rented for a year by Galen and Elizabeth Delaney. He commutes to Lexington where he is a Vice President of a bank and Elizabeth continues her sabbatical from being a Psychologist and recently successful author. Elizabeth just can't help herself when it comes to solving puzzles, everyday or abnormal.

Number 2. Hattie Griffin, housekeeper to the late Emily Caine, and nanny to both George Tate and Charles Simmons, has the house for her lifetime.

Number 3. Jenny and Joel Anderson live in the home given her by the Colonel when her parents were killed in a car accident. Though Jenny received some emotional healing, more is needed.

Number 4. George and Linda Tate and their children Reggie and Chuck enjoy their home and won't move no matter what they own. But could their children be in serious danger, even there in the gated community?

Number 5. Charles and Mindy Simmons are expecting a baby but have no idea the effect this has on one of their favorite couples in Tapestry Court.

Number 6. Bill Sinclair is Mindy's brother and a very busy employee for Tapestry Industries.

Number 7. Harold and Lucy Fowler have never really retired from ministry. How can they with so much need in Tapestry Court? And danger - which Harold is the first to suspect.

Chapter One

Elizabeth Daily-Delaney wiped the sweat off her brow and then wished she hadn't. That last batch of weeds she pulled looked suspiciously like Poison Oak.

She hurried into the house and with hands, arms, and face all washed and dried, she relaxed. Coming down the stairs, she remembered the first time she descended the steps at Number One Tapestry Court, the Manor House as it was called. Everything was clean and gleaming and she had paused to put a fingerprint on the banister to claim the place as her territory! *Unbelievable that it was only a few months ago. And everything has changed!*

Emily Caine, the one responsible for ensuring the house's pristine condition, died of heart failure, George Tate was declared the owner of Tapestry Industries, and Elizabeth married Galen Delaney.

She glanced down to see her watch and realized she left it upstairs on the counter of the master bathroom when she washed her hands.

On her way through the bedroom that she now shared with Galen, she smiled. The green and gold decorations made a person feel regal. She would always be grateful to Emily Caine for the decorations and upkeep of what was now her home. *At least for a while*. They were going to stay here until the expiration of the lease on the Manor House next spring. Then they'd decide what to do next. Her condo and his house in Lexington were sitting empty and that seemed a waste. The house would come in handy if Galen needed to stay over in Lexington, or if they had guests come in again, like his family did for their wedding. She considered renting her condo out, but the thought of a stranger there with all her possessions was just too much...and she didn't want to move them here in case they decided to move back to Lexington soon.

The watch revealed that Galen should be home in about forty-five minutes. Her heart leapt. Galen was the most wonderful, handsome, intelligent, funny, loving, and perfect man that ever lived. *In My Honest Opinion!*

By the time he walked in from the parking garage, Elizabeth had sugar snap peas ready to throw in the wok and the chicken tenders and mushrooms simmering in broth awaiting cornstarch. The rice packet was already in a glass casserole covered with water and would be perfect after twelve minutes in the microwave.

They ran toward each other almost like couples in a commercial, and kissed in a way they would not have dared a month earlier. The celibacy of their courtship made the fulfillment of their marriage a complete joy with no regret or guilt to mar it.

Today was their first day apart since the wedding twelve days ago. Their first night together was spent here and then they enjoyed a week at Laury's On the Lake outside of Simpsonton. The honeymoon ended on Wednesday and today Galen returned to work in Lexington where he was one of the vice presidents of a large bank.

After dinner Galen helped her wash the dishes and they went out to sit on the patio, their favorite spot. From there they could see over the small bushes and flowers in the patio garden back to the walled area that had been dubbed 'The Secret Garden' by eleven year old Chuck

Tate, who loved the Manor House and its surrounding property as much as Elizabeth and Galen did.

Galen broke the peaceful silence. "Well, I have some good news and some bad news."

Elizabeth frowned. "What?"

"First, the good news, construction on the addition to the garage will begin next Monday." The garage with its individual slots for the Tapestry Court residents was inadequate since it had been built at a time when the average family had only one car and one of the residents of Tapestry Court didn't drive at all. Now with the younger couples living there and the Tate children approaching driving age within a few years, several new places were needed.

"And the bad news?"

Galen grimaced. "It's really bad news. I have to leave Sunday afternoon for Boston. For two weeks."

Elizabeth's heart fell. "Can't I go with you?"

"They've booked the tickets for Jim Thompson and me. I checked but that flight is full. And to tell you the truth, I don't think I'll have any free time while I'm there. We'll be working on a loan participation with several other banks and also coordinating with the bank that provides our correspondent services."

"What's that mean?" Elizabeth asked.

"It has to do with technology, credit/debit, and securities."

"Oh." Elizabeth wasn't any wiser but she didn't really care. All she could think of was the very long two weeks without the love of her life.

They looked at each other with sadness.

***

Harold Fowler smiled when he saw that it was Reggie Tate waiting at the door of his home, Number Seven Tapestry Court.

"Come on in here!"

The teen paused to hug him. "Hi, Uncle Harold."

He could tell that it was still awkward for her to call him that. It had only been a few weeks since the relationship was discovered. All the years of her life until then, he and Lucy had been Reverend and Mrs. Fowler to the Tate children.

"Hello, my favorite niece!" He laughed and hugged her back. "Lucy! Guess who's here?"

Lucy Fowler came from the kitchen and beamed when she saw the girl.

"Reggie! I'm so glad to see you. Is there something you need?"

Reggie went over and hugged her Great Aunt. Then she turned around and included Harold in the request.

"I wanted to know if it would be wrong to ask for prayer for an audition."

"Audition?" Harold knew school was out. *What could the child be auditioning for?*

"The community theatre is putting on a production of 'The Wizard of Oz.' Kids are supposed to just audition for Dorothy or Toto or Munchkins or Flying Monkeys. But I'm too old for Dorothy and I don't want to be a Munchkin or a Monkey. I didn't want to be Toto, the dog, either so I'm glad I'm too big for that part. I want to play the part of the Glinda the Good." She took a deep breath.

Harold felt relief for her when she took in air. The girl talked so fast it almost made him breathless.

"They've got some famous lady from New York to play the Wicked Witch of the West and all the other grown up parts are for men. So...would it be wrong to ask God to give me that part, the part of Glinda?"

Lucy suggested they go into the living room. When they were all seated, the females looked at Harold for his assessment of God's interest in theatrical auditions.

I wish I had all the answers that people assume I have. Harold cleared his throat. "Since we don't know the will of God concerning the people who will be in this show, I think it would be better to pray another way."

Reggie's shoulders drooped but Harold was undaunted.

"We need to pray according to His will and I know it's His will that you do your best. And also that the ones choosing who will play which roles will look with favor on you."

"Cast." Reggie mumbled.

"Cast?" Harold asked.

"That's what it's called when they choose who will play the roles. They cast the play."

Harold nodded. "Cast. So, shall we all pray for that?"

Reggie agreed. He could tell that she would rather he asked God to make her be cast as Glinda the Good but he just couldn't do that.

The three joined hands as Harold led them to the throne of grace. "Father, I know how much you love Reggie and I ask that you give her favor in the eyes of those who make the decisions, those who cast the play. She wants to play Glinda but if you have a better plan, then cause them to make that decision. And Lord, I ask that you help Reggie do her very best at the audition. Amen."

Then before the others could move, he added. "And Lord, keep Reggie safe all during this time. We claim your protection for her, and thank you that you set angels round about her to protect her in all her ways. Protect her - spirit, soul, and body. Amen."

Lucy raised her head and gave him a strange look.

No wonder. That last part was you, Lord, not me. He shrugged his shoulders and grimaced at his wife.

***

Linda Tate looked at her stubborn eleven year old son through narrowed eyes. "Charles, it is not going to hurt you to take a couple of hours to come and see what's going on. You might get interested. And if you don't - well, it won't have hurt you!"

She could tell that Charles was trying not to duplicate her look because he knew he would get in trouble for being smart aleck if he did. Finally he sighed.

"Okay. I don't want to but I'll go."

She hugged him. "Good."

Just then Reggie walked in the kitchen door. "Are you ready to go, Mom?"

"Just about. Your brother is going with us!"

Out of the corner of her eye, Linda caught the up-turned wrinkled nose her daughter gave her younger brother, and his answering sneer.

"Where have you been, Reggie?" Linda finished drying the last dish and put the dish towel away.

"I just went over to tell Aunt Lucy and Uncle Harold about the auditions."

Linda smiled and nodded. "I'm glad." She was pleased that the Fowlers had proven to be blood relations to her children. George was an orphan and her parents lived so far away. It was a good thing for the children to have a real tie with that generation.

She saw Chuck roll his eyes toward heaven and could almost hear his thought that Reggie was trying to become their favorite.

The Tate family was not the first to arrive at the Library. A woman Linda had never seen before stood at the entrance directing people down the stairway to their right. The librarian, Glenda Taylor, waited at the bottom of the steps to greet them.

"I'm so glad you came." She nodded at Linda and Reggie. "And who's this?"

Linda answered. "This is my son, Charles. I thought he might find something he would be interested in doing. But he doesn't want to be one of the actors."

Glenda laughed. "That's great. I mean, usually everybody wants to act. We have a real need for stage crew. I hope you decide to join us." She smiled at Charles.

The librarian directed them to the table where Lisa Coulter, a local teacher, was receiving audition papers and dividing them into categories. Linda and Reggie handed her the ones they picked up at the library and already filled out.

"Would you like to fill out one?" The teacher looked at Charles.

"No, ma'am." He shook his head and stared at the floor.

"Oh! I wanted to ask a question." Linda looked back toward the librarian, but Glenda Taylor was greeting another family. She turned again to Lisa Coulter. "I've signed up to help with costumes but do you know if they will be made or rented?"

"You'll need to talk to Glenda later. I know she is planning on having a meeting just with those involved with the technical aspects sometime next week. But from what I understand some will be made and some rented."

Linda nodded. "Thanks."

***

When the children's parts - flying monkeys, Munchkins, Toto and Dorothy - had all been auditioned for, Carolyn Simpson Brock followed her daughter Margaret as they ascended the steps with the other dismissed parents and children. But before they went through the door which would automatically lock behind them, she stopped.

"Oh Margaret, Mom's left her sweater on the chair. We'll have to go back down."

She didn't like the look that Margaret gave her.

"I'll go get it for you."

"Oh, no. We'll both go."

When they got back down the stairs, Glenda was calling for those who were interested in the part of Glinda the Good. Three teen age girls joined her on the stage.

Carolyn whispered to Margaret. "Let's just sit down and watch. This will be good experience for you." She refused to acknowledge Margaret's sigh and pout.

The three teens were given scripts and asked to take turns reading different lines, some of Glinda's lines and some of Dorothy's.

Carolyn's stomach tightened. *Surely they are not going to choose Dorothy from those teenagers. Dorothy should be younger.*

Margaret tugged on her sleeve. "Come on, Mom. Let's go."

Carolyn shrugged the hand away and shook her head. "Not yet."

***

Ron Lockland breathed a sigh of relief when the younger children and their parents left. *What a bore! This whole thing is beyond boring. But if it gets Hannah here it's worth it.*

He was going to have to help cast so he paid attention to the three teenagers on stage. There was obviously only one who had any acting talent at all. She had potential and might be good in some future productions. *REAL shows. I wonder who this Cal person is that Hannah is bringing with her.* Since Ron was the stage manager, he would be working with the Technical Director very closely and hoped it would not be too difficult, hoped there was no romantic involvement between him and Hannah. *Hanley! Hanley! I've got to remember that. Not Hannah any more, Hanley! This time I've got to make it happen. I've just got to!*

***

Chuck couldn't help being proud of his sister. She was pretty good. The others were horrible. Well they were horrible reading those parts. They weren't bad at singing. He hated to admit it but Mom was right. He was kind of interested in the show. He'd never liked the movie "The Wizard of Oz" but it might be more interesting in person or whatever you called it.

The main thing that captured his attention was the brief announcement after the auditions that they really hoped for more people to sign up to help with sets and technical things. Ms. Taylor introduced Brandon Cress and said that he would be in charge of sound and lights. Mr. Cress seemed like a nice guy, and sound and lights sounded interesting.

Ms. Taylor also introduced Ron Lockland who would be the Stage Manager. He was a kind of skinny wimpy looking guy. She explained, "When the show goes up, the Director's job is over and the Stage Manager is in complete control. He will need people to change sets between scenes." That didn't sound too bad either but Chuck thought he'd rather work under Mr. Cress.

He signed a paper before they left. And saw his mother trying to hide the smile on her face.

***

Reggie was excited. She knew she'd done well, better than the others. She wondered why no grown women had auditioned for the part of Glinda the Good. She also wondered why they had her read some of Dorothy's lines. She was way too grown up to play Dorothy. She felt a pang of regret that she had not been able to be in plays when she was younger.

Glenda Taylor was talking again.

"We didn't have many adults audition, as you who are left can see. So we who are already in the theatre group will probably take those parts. But if you know anyone else who might be interested, please have them contact me. Thank you for coming out. The list will be posted tomorrow after five on the front door of the library. And I hope to see you Sunday afternoon when Hanley Drew will be in from New York to meet the cast and crew." She paused to acknowledge the smiles and nods from those gathered. "She'll be bringing a professional technical director with her too." She looked down at the notebook in her hand. "Cal Morgan. He's worked for some pretty well-known Broadway productions so we're very fortunate to have him."

When Reggie and her family got up to leave they saw that Carolyn Simpson Brock and her daughter were at the back of the room. Mrs. Brock walked over to Glenda Taylor, and Reggie could hear their conversation.

"Excuse me. I noticed that you had the older girls read some of Dorothy's lines. Does this mean that you are considering them too for that role?"

Glenda Taylor's face betrayed no emotion. "No. I just wanted to see how much variety they were capable of."

Margaret was pulling on her mother's arm, obviously anxious to leave but Mrs. Brock continued.

"I noticed that Crenshaw child was not bad when she tried out as a Munchkin. It's a shame that her family is so undependable. I just thought I'd drop a word to the wise!" She smiled and turned to leave.

Reggie could see by the look on the younger girl's face that Margaret was embarrassed at her mother's words.

That must be what they mean by a stage mother!

She leaned over and hugged her own mom.

***

When Linda Tate and her children left the meeting, another teenage girl walked out with them. Reggie introduced Sara Conley to her mother and brother.

"How are you getting home, Sara?" Linda asked when they reached her car.

"Oh, I'll walk. My mom works second shift. I'll be glad when I can drive."

Linda asked, "Where do you live? We'd be happy to give you a ride."

"Calvert Heights."

Linda was shocked. Calvert Heights was a low income apartment complex several miles away from the library. She couldn't imagine allowing Reggie to walk that distance at night alone.

"Well, hop in."

When they reached the housing complex, it was necessary to maneuver through a crowd of boys who were playing ball in the middle of the street. Some of them were smoking and a few made ugly gestures at the car. But they finally got Sara delivered safely to her front door.

Linda and her children were all quiet as they headed back toward Tapestry Court. Finally Charles spoke up. "Some of those guys are in my class at school."

"Yeah," Reggie agreed. "Mine too.

"Sara seems like a nice girl," Linda said. "Is she a friend of yours at school? I've never heard you mention her."

"No, not really. But maybe we might become friends." Reggie spoke in a weak voice that made Linda wonder if there was something about Sara she was not telling.

She knew that Reggie experienced a tough time the past few years because the girls she had been friends with in grade school were all dating and in a different world. Reggie had always been something of a loner and the older she got, the worse that tendency seemed to grow.

Thankfully, Reggie was interested in the church youth group and glad she was going to church camp over the summer. They had gotten permission from Glenda for her to miss rehearsals that week of camp which was three weeks before opening. Reggie would be back the same week that Hanley Drew returned to begin her own rehearsals.

Linda passed the gate to Tapestry Court and turned left into the long driveway that led to the parking garage. She was glad to get home but even more glad to get her children safely home. Away from the world of kids who smoke and make crude gestures. *Maybe I'll look into private school. We can afford it now!*

***

Elizabeth sighed as she pulled the car into the parking garage late that Sunday afternoon. Galen was now on the plane headed to...she looked at the clock on the dashboard. No, he was already in Charlotte, North Carolina where he would have to wait for over an hour before the next leg of his journey. It never ceased to amaze her that flights were so bizarre and did things like go south from Louisville, Kentucky in order to get north to Boston, Massachusetts.

She missed Galen already; it was going to be a long two weeks.

She walked through the park and decided to sit on a bench for a few minutes before going on to the house. It was so peaceful there in the Court, especially after the city traffic and hectic activity of the airport. And she dreaded going back home alone. It was going to seem awfully empty without her new husband.

She thought about visiting one of her neighbors but rejected the idea. That wouldn't be the same either with Galen not there. *What is wrong with me? I had no problem visiting alone a month ago. This 'one flesh' business can be carried too far!*

Just then her cell phone rang. She fished it out of her pocket and smiled when she saw that it was Galen calling.

"Just thought I'd let you know the first flight went fine and I'm sure the second one will too. Jim and I are getting ready to get something to eat."

"You'll call me when you get to Boston?"

"Of course. I'll call you when we land, and I'll call you from the hotel and give you the number of my room."

"I miss you!"

"Good." He laughed and then said in a gentle voice, "I miss you too, Bits. Take care of yourself."

"I will. But all of a sudden I can't think of anything to do with my time."

He laughed again. "That's not like you at all, Mrs. Delaney."

"I know it. You've ruined me!"

"Jim's motioning for me to come on. Love you!"

"I love you too."

Elizabeth walked slowly back to her home and let herself in the kitchen door just as the house phone began ringing.

Linda Tate's voice was a welcome sound. "Hi, Elizabeth. You're home from taking Galen to the airport?"

"I just walked in the door."

"Would you like to have supper with us? We've got tons of spaghetti left over from last night."

"Yes, I think I would. It feels awfully lonely around here."

Linda laughed softly. "I thought it might. See you in a few minutes?"

"I'll be there."

The males of the Tate family were unusually quiet. But Elizabeth realized that was because Linda and Reggie were unusually talkative. They were really excited about the Community theater production they were involved in. The first official meeting had been that afternoon.

"Mom's in charge of costuming. Mostly she just has to order from a costumer in Lexington."

"But then I'm in charge of making alterations for all of those. And – I have lots of children's Munchkin costumes to supervise – make sure the parents get them done in time – and make Glinda the Good's dress." She smiled at her daughter.

"I only have a couple of scenes but there just aren't any other good roles for girls my age." Despite her words, Elizabeth could tell that Reggie was proud of her part in the play.

Linda looked thoughtfully at Elizabeth. "Why don't you come with us to rehearsal Tuesday night? It would give you something to do while Galen's gone."

Elizabeth started to turn down the offer but stopped before the words reached her lips. *She's right. It would give me something to do.*

"Well, maybe. Yes! I think I'd like that. It would help me meet more people in town too. If we're going to live here, I guess I should know about something other than Tapestry Court and church...and the library."

"The librarian, Glenda Taylor, is our director," Reggie announced with a smile. "She's a really nice lady."

Elizabeth nodded. "I met Glenda at the library. I like her."

"Yes, I like her too," Linda added. "I don't know if you get the paper..."

Elizabeth shook her head. "No, I admit that I am not a newspaper fan."

Before Linda could continue, Reggie broke in. "It was in the paper. The best thing is that the Wicked Witch of the West is going to be played by a real actress from New York. She was there today and she's awesome. She said we are sisters." Then she turned to her mother. "I keep forgetting to ask you...what did she mean when she said something about we'd have bigger parts if we were playing wicked or something. I didn't get it."

Linda laughed. "There was a popular Broadway show called 'Wicked' based on a book by the same name. It's supposed to be the true story of friendship between the Wicked Witch of the West and Glinda the Good."

Reggie nodded. "Got it!"

Linda turned back to Elizabeth. "Hanley Drew is from Simpsonton - her name used to be Hannah. She was pretty popular in high school, went off to college to study drama and had a break one summer in New York. The rest is history."

Elizabeth nodded. She noticed that Chuck was watching her reactions to his mother and sister so she addressed him. "So, Chuck, what are you doing this summer?"

"Well, I'm going to help with the play some." He straightened up in his chair and she saw the old sure-of-himself boy she first met. "I'm part of the Tech crew. I'll be helping build sets and also changing props and stuff during the ... well, when the real play is going on."

"Performances." Reggie didn't actually smirk but Elizabeth could tell she was glad to know the correct terminology.

"Whatever," Chuck said. Then he turned to Elizabeth again. "I wanted to run lights and sound but they said they needed me more for stage crew." His face brightened. "But Mr. Cress, the light guy, said he'd teach me and maybe in another play I can do that."

"That's great, Chuck."

Suddenly the boy turned to his father. "Dad, now that Uncle Charles is going to get his own kid, couldn't everybody please call me Chuck?"

The adults all laughed. And Reggie rolled her eyes.

George smiled at his son and nodded. "Yes, Char...Chuck. I think it would be okay." Then he looked at Linda. "All right with you?"

Linda leaned over and hugged her son. "Yes, Chuck. It's fine with me."

Elizabeth felt a ridiculous satisfaction that she had been a part of the boy's wish coming true. And she recognized that there was a huge maternal part of her heart that had never been exercised. Not until the day she moved to Tapestry Court and met Chuck Tate.

George and both kids wandered off to watch TV while Elizabeth helped Linda clear the table.

"So tell me about the stars from New York."

Linda Tate frowned. "Strange. Hanley Drew is quite a professional, always on."

"Fake?"

Linda slowly shook her head. "Not exactly. She seems genuinely fond of the local people and considers this home. Especially you can tell she loves Lisa Coulter, the teacher. They grew up together. Lisa's parents died and Hannah's parents got custody, with the approval of a grandmother. Hanley. I've got to remember she's Hanley now instead of Hannah."

"So they were like sisters?"

Linda nodded.

Elizabeth pressed on. "So what did you mean about strange?"

"I'm not sure. There was just an atmosphere, something not right. Part of it was the two guys she brought with her from New York."

"Two? I thought you said just one was coming, a Technical Director."

"Yeah, but there are two of them. Cal Morgan, the Tech Director is - well Reggie called him 'a real hottie."

Both women grinned.

"Supposedly he and Hanley are an item."

Elizabeth was still smiling. "And the other?"

Linda fidgeted with the tea towel. "Well that's definitely one of the strange things. I'm not sure why he came but he really, well, it seems like he's in love with Cal Morgan too."

Elizabeth said the first thing that came to her mind. "Theatre people!"

***

The plan of the high school stage area lay there on the table. The script was to its right. The list of movements of every actor and stage crew for the crucial time was to the left of the plan. It's going to work. I'm sure it's going to work.

Chapter Two

Aleph, Bet, Gimmel, Dallet, Hey, Vav, Zayin... Harold Fowler looked up from the Hebrew Primer he gave in and bought last week in Lexington. Several months ago he remembered how he loved the year of studying Hebrew in Seminary and vowed then to learn it better some day. The years of missionary work in China and even more years later as a pastor put off that day until retirement. And then he forgot about it until recently.

To his dismay, when he pulled out the Hebrew textbook he used a half century ago he realized that the text he had once so delighted in now gave him a headache. It just wasn't the same without an enthusiastic professor there to spur you on. *And classmates to compete against? Surely not! Was I that prideful?*

So now he was starting over with a simplified workbook. But still, even with the learnable instruction, he couldn't seem to capture his original excitement and sense of adventure in learning the language of Moses and the prophets.

His vacant gaze finally focused in on the scene in the front window of his office. Reggie Tate was spreading a

blanket on the spot she obviously preferred for sunbath-
ing, between the Tate home and the house of Bill Sinclair.
He was glad she got the part she wanted in the play, but
the uncomfortable feeling that rose up in him the night
Reggie came to ask for prayer about auditions returned.

What was all that about protection for Reggie? Spirit,
soul, and body. I know you led that prayer Lord, but why?
It sounds like temptation as well as physical danger will try
to attack her.

With a sigh, he pushed the Hebrew primer toward the
back of the desk and got up from his chair.

"I'm going over to George's." He called in a loud voice
and then waited to make sure Lucy heard him from the
kitchen.

"Okay, dear!"

They always told each other when they went out of the
house. It began as a joke back when their son was in sixth
grade and came home one day to find no one there. Lucy
was actually out in the garage of the parsonage but Jackson didn't know that and when she came back in the
house she found her son sobbing hysterically.

"I thought the rapture had happened," He sobbed between each word. "And you and Daddy were gone with Jesus and I was here all alone." Lucy took him in her arms
and comforted him, and Harold promised that he would
not be left behind should Jesus come to take His people
away in Jackson's lifetime.

But for a while they made a point of informing each
other, with a grin, "I'm leaving now but not away from the
earth." Then it just got down to letting each other know if
they left the house and most of the time they didn't even
remember the origin of the courtesy.

Harold chuckled as he thought back on the good old
days. Then the ever-smothered sadness of the present
came back. He wished his son lived closer so they could
spend more time together.

Jackson followed his father's example and answered the call to ministry, but he far surpassed Harold in popularity. He was the senior pastor of a mega-church with little time for a personal life. He lived in Texas so Harold and Lucy rarely saw their son, daughter-in-law, or two grandsons.

Reggie was engrossed in a book when Harold crossed the walk to her side yard. She sensed his presence and looked up, and a smile spread across her face. "Hi, Uncle Harold."

He smiled back and then stared as he noticed her reading material. The cover was black and white and sickly green with a picture of a witch and the word WICKED in large letters.

She laughed as she saw him looking at the book. "This isn't what you think. It's a novel based on the life of Glinda the Good – that's me in the play– and the Wicked Witch of the West."

Harold was relieved. There was so much bad literature these days to pollute the minds of the young. But surely the fairy tales couldn't hurt.

"I was just curious how the play is going."

"It's fun," Reggie said. "We've only had two real rehearsals. Sunday and last night. Mrs. Delaney went with us last night." She grinned. "I don't have a big part but I got the one I wanted. And since I'm helping with the younger kids, I get to be at almost every rehearsal."

"And how does your brother like his job?"

Reggie wrinkled her nose. "Oh, him. He gets more and more bossy all the time. If a prop is moved a few inches, he makes sure to tell everybody how important it is to put everything in its place. And we don't even have the real props or sets yet."

"In other words, he likes it a lot." Harold laughed.

Reggie smiled. "Yeah, he's having fun. And good news that Mom got my church camp changed 'til the week after the performances so I don't have to miss any rehearsals at all."

Harold nodded. He didn't know how to talk to teenage girls. He and Lucy only had the one son and he was greatly relieved during his years as pastor that someone else managed the youth groups.

He didn't know what he wanted to say anyway.

"Well, if there's ever anything I can do to help – er – pray or anything, just let me know."

Reggie looked at him a little strangely but she nodded. "Okay, Rev...Uncle Harold."

***

The sound of machines drilling through concrete shattered the usual morning peace of Tapestry Court. Elizabeth finally moved from her favorite spot on the patio and took her Bible and notebook into the house. The move muffled the sound slightly but it soon became obvious that ear plugs were needed. She wondered how her neighbors were handling the unpleasant noise.

There was no question that the garage addition was needed and no one complained when all the vehicles had to be moved to the parking lot beside the Archer's grocery last night. Joe and Jane Archer were always very generous with their parking lot to Tapestry Court residents and their guests. They even closed the store and made a special sign for parking at their place for Galen and Elizabeth's wedding.

It was good that besides making more enclosed spaces in the parking garage, there would be several pavement spaces for guests beside the garage. A communication system would be installed so guests could phone the home they were visiting and the household could release the locked gate to the park.

George Tate insisted on paying for the new amenities himself. He told Elizabeth and Galen that he was still in a slight state of shock at finding himself the owner of the vast Tapestry fortune. But there was no doubt of his generosity and desire to share his wealth with his family and friends.

After retrieving ear plugs from the upstairs bathroom, Elizabeth settled herself on the couch in the parlor and picked up her Bible again. The parlor was the room that was most distant from the construction site. But after a very short time she gave up.

"Okay, Lord. You and I will have to meet later. I can't hear You for the racket!"

After filling her coffee mug, she let herself out her front door, left the Manor House property and went down the walkway to Number #5 Tapestry Court where Mindy and Charles Simmons lived.

Mindy opened the door and immediately a big smile spread across her face.

"Elizabeth! Come in. I'm so glad to see you." Then almost immediately. "Isn't this noise awful?"

"Yes! I couldn't concentrate at the house." She grinned. "I thought maybe the Andersons house in between might make yours more soundproof. I wonder how long that will last?"

"I have no idea. But maybe George can find out and give us an estimate."

"You know, it is a little better here. Not much, but a little."

"You came at a good time," Mindy said. "I've just finished sorting out your mail."

Elizabeth felt a stirring in her stomach. *I don't want to think about my mail.*

Mindy continued. "I've got the invitations for speaking engagements in one pile." She gave a small apologetic shrug. "Most of them are months old and really need to be answered as soon as possible."

Elizabeth knew she had been abominably rude in the area of the mail. When her book, Reconciling *The Old and New Testament Images of God*, was contracted and renamed *The Fall and Redemption of God* by the publishers, the results of the sales had sent her into a state of shock from which she wasn't entirely recovered.

She found herself incapable of responding to the fan mail as well as the hate mail. And the requests for speaking engagements made her want to run and hide. When she finally hired Mindy Simmons as a secretary to handle that part of her life over a month ago, she breathed a sigh of relief and put the matter out of her mind.

Now she breathed a different kind of sigh and resigned herself to face the responsibility.

"Okay, what do I need to do?"

Mindy laughed. "It's not that bad. I can do most of the work. You are just going to have to decide which places you are willing to go and when. I've already drawn up several drafts of form letters for your approval as responses to some of the other letters."

Elizabeth nodded. "Wonderful. But I'm not about to make any decisions about speaking until Galen is home to help me figure out dates."

"Fair enough. Come on into the office." Mindy led the way to the downstairs room that exactly corresponded with Harold Fowler's office.

Elizabeth was impressed. Mindy had taken her boxes of unopened mail as well as the wire crates of those that she had begun sorting. The latter had been enough to send Elizabeth into the swivet that resulted in her taking a sabbatical from her practice as a psychologist and fleeing to Simpsonton and Tapestry Court to sort out her life instead. Now Mindy had the letters all open and stapled to the envelopes they came in. There were five large piles in boxes with a typewritten page on the top of each pile: Complaints, Compliments, Invitations, Needs, Questions.

Elizabeth nodded in appreciation of the orderliness.

"See, that's not so bad, is it?" Mindy looked at her anxiously.

Elizabeth took a sip from her coffee cup. "No, not at all. You've done a very good job. I'm impressed."

Mindy grinned. "I was a great secretary. That's what I do best. Hey, do you want to stay in here to look at the drafts, or settle at the kitchen table? I've got a pot of coffee on."

"I don't need any more coffee but the kitchen table sounds comfortable. It won't seem as businesslike as in here." She waved vaguely at the piles of letters.

Elizabeth saw no changes to make on the drafts created to answer the complaint or compliment letters. But they agreed that she would personally need to dictate the ones that contained questions or expressed needs. And then of course there were the speaking requests.

Mindy said, "Whenever and however you want to handle the dictation is fine with me. I guess you have lots of time this week with Galen gone. I kept meaning to call but was busy getting this done. And then when Charles comes in from work..." She blushed. Elizabeth was so happy for Mindy that her marriage had turned a corner and was now the happy and fulfilling relationship that she had long desired.

"I mean, Charles is still Charles. He's probably never going to be really romantic or anything but I know he loves me and we really are happy." She patted her stomach. "And we have the little one to thank. We might have gone through life miserable and keeping secrets if it weren't for him, or her."

Elizabeth felt another pang inside. Mindy was getting ready to experience something that she had never known. And never would.

Mindy reached out and took her hand. "You know, Elizabeth, this child will not have any grandparents because of Charles and me both being orphans but it will have you and Galen. That makes me so happy."

Elizabeth hoped she kept her face from showing the dismay she felt at Mindy's words. Once when she first met Bill Sinclair she judged him to be much younger and thought he might be the age to be her son. She discovered later with relief that since he was thirty-two, she would have had to have been thirteen when he was born. But that did not apply to his sister who was seven years younger. *I could be Mindy's mother!*

"We are so happy for you." Elizabeth really meant it and hoped her voice did not sound as hollow as her emotions felt.

The drilling sound ceased abruptly and Elizabeth stood up. "I really need to get back now." She leaned down to hug Mindy. "You are a real blessing to me in a lot of ways."

"And you to me."

She left with promises to set a date to sign letters as soon as Mindy had them ready and to begin dictation as soon as that first task was accomplished. Then she turned back just as Mindy was closing the door.

"But you know there are probably more letters being held at the Lexington Post Office."

"Yes." Mindy nodded. "I figured that. But...sufficient unto the day is the mail thereof!"

Elizabeth laughed and started walking back to #1. Then she changed her mind, turned, and went to the house directly across from Mindy's.

Linda Tate welcomed her in with glass cleaner in one hand and paper towels in the other. "Hey! I was going to call you in a few minutes. Are you still coming to rehearsal with us again tomorrow night?"

Elizabeth nodded. "Yes, I actually came to ask if there is anything useful I can do."

Linda's eyes lit up. "Yes! I need help measuring the cast. I want to get started as soon as possible on costumes. We've got some to order and some to make. I've got to choose patterns for the one I make for Reggie, and the ones I give to the parents to make or have made."

"Okay. Count me in. Just tell me what to do. And even after Galen gets back I can help in the daytime when he's at work." Elizabeth started to turn away and then turned back.

Linda tilted her head and looked at her. "Elizabeth, is something wrong?"

Elizabeth felt tears spring to her eyes. "Got a minute?"

Soon they were seated in Linda's kitchen with a pot of tea and some bagels and cream cheese on the table between them.

"I know I'm silly. And I'm not upset with her, really! But Mindy just told me that she was glad her baby would have Galen and me since they wouldn't have any real grandparents. It's a compliment but..."

Linda reached across the table and squeezed Elizabeth's hand.

"Oh, I totally understand. I remember when Reggie got her period, I realized I could be a grandmother. It was a horrible thought."

"The really horrifying thing is that I *am* old enough to be Mindy's mother. I was twenty when she was born." She paused and then went on.

"And what makes it worse is that for the first time in my life I'm beginning to feel like I wish I had children. It started with Chuck. I enjoy him so much. And then when I went with you last night, the little Munchkins were so cute...Hmm." She laughed and glared at Linda through narrowed eyes. "Chuck, the Munchkins – this emotional storm is all your fault!"

Linda laughed too. "I've got broad shoulders." Then she got sober. "But why not? I mean have you had a hysterectomy or anything?"

Elizabeth shook her head. "No but..."

"But what? Women have children at ... how old are you?"

"Forty five."

"Women have children in their forties all the time. And you're happily married. It's not too late!"

Elizabeth just stared at her friend.

What on earth would Galen feel about having a baby?

Finally she found her voice. "Well you pray about it and I'll pray about it. And if I'm still feeling this way when Galen gets home, I'll talk to him."

Linda nodded.

About the time Elizabeth left to go back to the Manor House, the drilling began again.

Elizabeth enjoyed the rehearsals much more than she thought she would. Some of the little ones were really funny in their roles as Munchkins. One girl was determined to get a boy to hold hands with her even though he pulled his hand away every time she grabbed it. At one point he ran all over the stage, ducking through other Munchkins, with his wanna-be girl friend in hot pursuit.

This is a part of life I missed out on. Again, some long buried maternal instinct poked its head up and insisted on being recognized. The children were so cute. She loved just watching them. They didn't care what anybody thought or even notice if anyone was looking. They just lived in the moment and ignored the world around them unless forced to attention by an adult. *How refreshing.*

Elizabeth had not been around children since the hours spent while she was working on her Master's Degree. The Doctoral program had not required her to do any practicum outside her own field. *Probably why I collect castles and love tea parties. I was deprived of a big part of the magic in life.*

After the smaller children and their parents left, Reggie could have gone too, since the opening Munchkin scene was the only one Glinda the Good was in for this rehearsal. But Chuck needed to work with the tech crew so the Tate family stayed and Elizabeth stayed with them.

The only other children there were Margaret Brock, who was playing Dorothy, and a Munchkin child who sat with her own mother, watching the stage. Linda said that

Margaret's some-degree-great-grandparent was the Simpson who founded Simpsonton.

The three Tapestry Court females sat together watching the rehearsal as Dorothy, the Tin Man, Scarecrow, and Cowardly Lion went through several scenes. Since there were no costumes as yet, the characters of the trio of companions were conveyed completely by the talent of the actors. Elizabeth watched with fascination as the good looking young actor walked about awkwardly and by his movements and stilted speech managed to convey that he was a Tin Man.

She also noticed that Reggie Tate was staring at the Tin Man. A warning bell went off inside her mind. *That look isn't just fascination with good acting. This looks like the beginnings of a crush...but he is in his late twenties at least – way too old for Reggie.*

She would have to find out who the good looking young man was in real life.

The Scarecrow concerned her for another reason. The young woman playing that part was trying very hard to act as though she had no bones but the director kept stopping her.

"Scarecrow, you need to loosen up! You're still looking stiff."

The Scarecrow nodded but didn't get any looser. Elizabeth felt sorry for her. There was something about her that reminded her of a client from when she was in practice as a psychologist. She just couldn't put her finger on which client or what the something was.

The Cowardly Lion was funny. He lumbered awkwardly all over the stage and stuck his fingers in his mouth and acted all goofy just like a cowardly lion should.

The child sitting in the audience with her mother clapped after every line he spoke and it was obvious that the Lion was the Munchkin's daddy.

On their way to the car, Elizabeth casually mentioned the Tin Man. "He was very good. Who is he?"

Before Linda could open her mouth, Reggie answered with enthusiasm. "He is David Sutton. He's the youth director at First Baptist Church. Isn't he ... talented?"

Elizabeth relaxed. *Ah, a youth director. Surely he will know how to handle teen adoration.*

"And who is the Scarecrow?"

At that question Reggie frowned. "Ms. Coulter. She's a fourth grade teacher. She's weird."

Elizabeth remembered Linda telling her about the teacher growing up with Hanley Drew's family.

Linda reproved her daughter. "Reggie! You didn't even have her in school. You don't know her and it's not nice to call her weird."

Elizabeth saw Chuck and Reggie exchange a look. *Well, that's the first thing I've ever seen them in agreement about. Ms. Coulter must be at least a little weird!*

But then being orphaned and raised by others who are not family can do that to you. As she well knew!

Elizabeth rode again with the Tates to the Saturday afternoon rehearsal of 'The Wizard of Oz.' Linda said that at this point there would only be three rehearsals a week, Tuesday and Thursday nights, and Saturday afternoon.

Simpsonton was very much a church oriented town so Wednesday night and Sunday rehearsals would be frowned on. Later, closer to the performances, Monday and Friday nights would be added.

The time was fun for Elizabeth again, but always niggling at the back of her mind was a longing to see Galen.

Elizabeth shocked herself by enjoying answering the 'needs' correspondence from the letters. It wasn't quite the same as in-person counseling, but it filled a need in her. Especially now when she felt so needy herself. And she had to smile at all the 'need' words coming to mind.

How would she bring up the question of a baby to Galen? And why was she so nervous about it. Surely he would want a child of his own. A child of their own. *Our baby. Oh, please, Lord!*

***

Reggie did some quick math in her head. She was sixteen and Pastor Sutton was twenty-eight; she'd looked in the theater files at his application. Twelve years difference. That wasn't really a lot. She thought she remembered that Uncle Charles and Mindy were almost that far apart in age. But they were older when they met. Maybe it would be some kind of a crime for David...she blushed as she called him that in her mind... to date her until she turned eighteen. Two whole years!!!

So strange, she'd never been interested in boys before. Still wasn't, she reminded herself. David Sutton was a man.

***

There could be a glitch. The underlined people on the cast/crew list might be a problem. But surely the gods would protect.

Chapter Three

"Absolutely not!"

Elizabeth felt herself draw back involuntarily. The look on Galen's face was frightening.

It was as if she was with a stranger, not the man she loved and had given her life to. Maybe she should have waited until he'd been home a few days instead of hitting him with this after two weeks apart.

"Have you lost your mind?" Then his mouth and eyes relaxed slightly. "Is this a menopause thing?"

Fear gave way to anger. "No! It's not. I haven't started into menopause yet. I'm perfectly capable of getting pregnant and having a baby."

"Well, it's not going to happen!" The narrowed eyes and glare returned.

She was trembling inside and not sure of the source. Anger? Fear? Shock?

Sorrow? But she forced herself to speak.

"What is wrong with you, Galen Delaney? You have never spoken to me in that tone of voice. Or looked at me with that kind of look on your face."

His expression didn't change but he shook his head. "Sorry." And then he scooted his chair back and left her sitting at the patio table alone.

Elizabeth couldn't stop the tears that sprang to her eyes. It felt like a nightmare and she'd wake up soon. But it wasn't. This horrible scene was a real part of her life, her marriage.

The psychologist part of her mind whispered 'this is something deeply emotional for him, something from the past.' But she could barely hear the whisper for the screaming pain of the wife part.

She wanted to do something, go after him, talk it out. But she couldn't move and just sat there paralyzed.

**

It was only two more weeks until Hanley Drew would be back for the weeks of increased rehearsals and the performances. Reggie finished reading Wicked and it was okay but she was much more impressed with David Sutton. She wanted to ask Sara what she thought about it, what she would do. She'd heard rumors around the school for years that Sara ... well, she didn't have a very good reputation. They said she 'did it' with boys. Reggie didn't want to 'do it' but she'd like to find out more about how to act with guys.

**

Linda Tate knocked on the door of Number Seven and bit her nails while she waited for one of her newly discovered in-laws to answer. It was Lucy Fowler who came, and the polite smile on her face grew into joy when she saw who was there. Linda's heart warmed at the visible proof of acceptance and love. She had been going to talk just to Reverend Fowler - she didn't think she could ever call him 'Uncle Harold' - but she changed her mind about talking only to him before she spoke.

"I wondered if I could talk to you and Reverend Fowler for a few minutes. If you have time, I mean." She didn't want them to think she thought of them as always available because of nothing to do.

Lucy laughed. "Are you kidding? We'd love to visit with you. Tea?"

Linda nodded and Lucy led her into the kitchen. "I'll put the pot on and go get Harold. Have a seat? Or would you rather talk in the living room?"

"Here is fine," Linda said. She looked around at the kitchen, just like hers in the basics, but decorated completely differently. It was uniquely Lucy Tapestry Fowler.

There were shelf upon shelf of teapots and teacups. Some were formal, some fun, some British, some Asian. Minnie Mouse and Cinderella sat next to Blue Willow and California Ivy. The cabinets, which in her own house were natural wood, were painted white with blue trim and matched the linoleum on the floor which was white with blue flowers.

By the time the teapot was whistling, Harold and Lucy returned. He acted no less pleased to see her than his wife.

Soon they were all seated around the table with teacups filled with strong tea.

Reverend Fowler said, "Did you know, Linda, that tea came from China originally?"

"No. I thought it was English."

"We did too. But when we were on the mission field we found out that the western world has only known about it for about four hundred years though it's been used in China for over four thousand." He laughed. "We westerners think we know everything. It's humbling to find out how much we owe to other nations."

Linda smiled and nodded. She really didn't know how to bring up the subject for which she came.

Lucy reached over and patted her arm. "Now, dear, what did you want to see us about?"

Linda's eyes filled with tears as she looked at the loving concern on both faces. "It's Elizabeth."

Lucy rose and picked up a box of tissues which sat on the sideboard. She handed one to Linda and set the rest on the table.

"This is so silly of me," Linda wiped the tears away as she spoke. "But you know, even though Elizabeth has only been here a few months, she is the friend I've always prayed for."

Reverend Fowler nodded. "We all love Elizabeth. She's like one of the family, fits in here as if she always belonged and we - and she - just didn't know it."

Linda smiled. "You understand then." She sighed. "And I don't know why I'm here and maybe I shouldn't be talking about it but... I want you two to pray for Elizabeth and Galen. Something is wrong."

Harold Fowler frowned. "Something wrong?"

Linda repeated what Elizabeth told her about wanting a baby and how they prayed together for the Lord to lead how Elizabeth should approach Galen. And then how Elizabeth had come to her house in tears to report Galen's reaction.

"That was a week ago. And she doesn't talk about it anymore but she's coming to all the rehearsals at night, which she said she wasn't going to do because she didn't want to leave Galen at night." Linda looked back and forth from one compassionate face to the other. "I asked her how things were going but she just said 'Fine' and changed the subject." Linda sighed and picked up her teacup. "I just don't know what to do."

"Let's pray," said Harold Fowler. And he did.

***

Elizabeth hung up the kitchen phone and turned to Galen who was seated with a cup of coffee at the head of the table. "The Fowlers want to know if we'd like to come for supper tomorrow night. I said I'd talk to you and call them back."

He didn't look up from the newspaper. "Aren't you going to be at your play?"

Elizabeth swallowed the lump in her throat that formed at his sarcastic tone of voice. "No, tomorrow's Wednesday. They don't have rehearsals on Wednesday." She went to the oven and pulled out the stuffed yellow peppers and set them on top of the stove. She sighed before pulling out two plates and their silverware and then wished she hadn't. Hopefully Galen hadn't heard her and thought she was trying to be dramatic.

While she set the table she asked, "What kind of salad dressing do you want, Sweetheart?"

He didn't answer. Elizabeth took a deep breath. "Galen!"

He slowly raised his head but stared at the ceiling.

"Galen, what is wrong? We can't go on like this. This isn't ... it isn't us. You've been my best friend, even before we were in love. What is wrong?"

He just shook his head.

"Why won't you look at me?" She could hear the pleading in her voice - and hated it.

Galen lowered his head but still didn't face her. "Look, Elizabeth. This is something I can't talk about. I'm sorry I've disappointed you. That I'm not what you wanted. I'm glad you've found something you are interested in - with the play." And he picked up the newspaper again. Then he mumbled, "French."

She stared at the back of the newspaper. "French?"

"French dressing will be fine."

Disbelief warred with irritation. "And what about the Fowlers? What do I tell them?"

"Might as well go. Nothing better to do."

She fought back the tears as she recalled how just a few weeks ago, neither of them wanted to do anything when he got home from work except delight in each other.

That hadn't happened since she asked him about the baby.

She couldn't help it; she still thought of 'the baby.' More than ever. His refusal to discuss it had made her desire even stronger. For someone to love who would love her unconditionally? What had happened to the competent professional who had life under control? She put the peppers on the plates and the salad in bowls.

"Supper's ready." She got the French dressing out of the refrigerator and set it in front of his salad bowl. He laid the paper down and picked up his knife and fork.

"Galen, I love you. You are exactly what I want. I'm sorry I upset you. I had no idea you felt that way about babies."

He looked at his plate. "No you wouldn't have any reason to know that. We never discussed it. I didn't think at our ages, the issue would ever come up." He took a bite of the stuffed pepper. "This is really good. What's in it?"

"Just hamburger, rice, tomato sauce, and garlic." Was that it? The end of the subject of the baby?

"I think I know what makes this better than other stuffed peppers. No green pepper. I don't like green peppers."

"Yes, the yellow or red ones are so much milder - don't have that bitter taste."

He ate everything on his plate without any more comments. But he did offer to help her with the dishes for the first time since their quarrel.

"That's all right, Sweetheart. You've had a long day. You go on and relax. And maybe when I finish we could have coffee together on the patio?"

He finally looked at her. And nodded. "That would be nice."

Elizabeth felt her muscles relax as he walked in the other room. Before she started on the dishes, she phoned the Fowlers and told them they would love to come for dinner the next night.

Then she called Linda and said she was sorry but she'd have to skip rehearsal tonight.

***

"Can I ask Sara home to spend the night?" Rehearsal had gone very well and Linda noticed the two teenage girls spending time giggling together when neither were on stage. That was good. Reggie needed friends her own age.

"Of course, but she'll need to get permission from her mother. Can she be reached by phone at her work?"

Her daughter gave her a quick hug. "I'll find out."

Linda didn't like where Sara lived, or that her mother was never around, but the girl herself seemed like a very polite, well behaved child. The Tates took her home after every rehearsal and Sara always thanked her as if it were the first time. That was good - the girl wasn't one of those people who took things for granted, no entitlement mentality.

The two teens joined Linda and Chuck at the entrance to the library.

"Yay! She can sleep over tonight, Mom!" Linda couldn't tell which of the girls looked happier. "But is it okay to go by her house so she can get some clothes?"

"Of course."

When they got to the apartment, and past the crude boys who always lined the streets, all the lights were on instead of just the front light that was usually shining to welcome the girl home to the empty house. Before they even got in front of the place, they could hear loud music pouring forth. But Linda could still hear the groan from the back seat.

"I'll be right back," Sara said in a subdued voice.

The three Tates sat there in silence while they waited. It was nearly ten minutes later that Sara came out with a woman that Linda supposed was her mother. But she wasn't dressed like a mother. Short shorts - no, short, short shorts - and a top that was more like a bandana. The woman came to the driver's side door and Linda rolled down her window.

"Thank you so mush for giving my baby rides and havin' her over. I rilly 'preshiate it." Linda stopped herself from drawing back at the scent of alcohol that blew into the car at the woman's words.

"You're welcome." Linda forced herself to smile. "Sara is a very nice girl. We enjoy her, Mrs. Conley."

Another blast of alcohol hit her in the face as Sara's mother laughed, a raucous laugh. "I ain't Mrs. Conley, or Mrs. anything. Sara's father was Conley but my name is Drake. Bee Drake." She stuck her hand in the window. "Glad to meesha."

Linda shook the woman's hand. "Linda Tate. Nice to meet you too, uh, Bee." She took a deep breath. "What time do you want Sara home tomorrow?"

Ms. Drake shook her head. "Don't matter." She nodded her head toward the apartment. "I got compny so it don't matter at all."

"Well then, I'll have her call you. We'd better be getting back now; it's getting late."

Sara's mother gave her a salute and turned away, almost tripped on the curb but caught herself and went on toward the house. Linda backed the car out of the parking place.

"I'm sorry." Sara's voice sounded very small and sad. "I didn't know she'd taken off work."

"But I thought you'd called her to get permission to spend the night."

"No ma'am. I was just going to leave a note telling her where I was." After a few seconds of silence, Sara spoke again. "I'm really sorry you saw her, especially like that. If you don't want Reggie to be friends with me, I understand."

Linda's heart tightened. "Sara, of course I want Reggie to be friends with you."

The rest of the trip home was traveled in silence. Even Chuck had nothing to say.

Linda parked the car at the Archer' grocery store lot and the kids started talking as they introduced Sara Conley to Tapestry Court.

"Wow, it's like something out of a movie." Sara seemed truly in awe, after commenting on the gas lanterns with their flickering lights, and the stone wall surrounding the entire Court, except for the gate.

Linda looked around in satisfaction. Sometimes you got used to things and forgot how blessed you were.

Reggie pointed straight ahead. "The Manor House is there, behind that far gate. I know Ms. Daily, uh, Mrs. Delaney would let us come and see it tomorrow. It's really neat."

"It has a great garden." Chuck added.

But Linda couldn't help but wonder what was going on inside the fairy tale exterior of Number One, Tapestry Court.

***

Elizabeth snuggled closer to her now gently snoring husband. *Thank you, Lord, we finally are back together.*

They hadn't talked about the baby anymore and Elizabeth told herself it didn't matter. Galen was all she needed in life. Besides God. And her new Tapestry Court family. They were going to have dinner with the Fowlers tomorrow night and that was almost like having parents. And Linda Tate was like a sister. And Mindy. Another sister?

Surely not a daughter? Her heart tightened again. *Lord, I'm old.* But then she recalled the past hour with Galen and giggled. *Okay. Not too old.*

***

"So, tell me about boys. I don't know any of them except my brother and he's so young and boring. But you know about them, don't you?"

They were sitting on Reggie's bed but Sara pulled the pillow over her face. "You've heard?" The words were muffled but Reggie was pretty sure that's what her friend said.

"Sara? I'm sorry. Shouldn't I have asked? I thought I could learn from you."

The pillow was thrust down and Sara's eyes were blazing. "No! You don't want to learn anything from me. I want to learn from you. Didn't you see my mother tonight? I don't want to end up like her. I want to be like you and your mother!"

"I'm sorry." Reggie knew she was repeating herself but she couldn't think of anything else to say.

Sara breathed a deep breath and her shoulders seemed to relax. "Okay - here it is. I've never had a real friend before - you're the closest thing to it. I don't want to drive you away but I guess I have to be honest."

"You won't drive me away, I promise." Reggie reached out and took Sara's hand.

***

Elizabeth closed her Bible and picked up her prayer journal from the patio table. She put them on the shelf in the library where she kept them and pulled out a stack of correspondence that she'd brought from Mindy's, just as the doorbell rang. She left the library and opened the door to see the smiling faces of Reggie Tate and her friend from the play, Sara.

"Come in." Elizabeth returned their smiles.

"We don't want to bother you, Mrs. Delaney." Reggie scrunched up her face. "I was just showing Sara around the Court and wondered if it's okay to show her your garden? And then sometime when it's convenient, maybe the Manor House?"

"It's fine now, Reggie. Come on in. In fact it's perfect timing. I hadn't started on some paper work I have to do yet." She opened the screen door and the girls entered the house.

She led them first into the parlor and the look on Sara's face made her heart melt.

"Oh, how pretty! This looks like something out of a movie, just like the whole place does from the outside."

Elizabeth laughed, "I can't take any credit for the decorations. They were here when I moved in."

They wandered through the rest of the house including the small spare room upstairs that Galen was turning into a part-time office.

As they were going down the steps, Reggie tripped and let out a shriek. She landed on the floor at the foot of the stairway and Elizabeth breathed a silent prayer of thanks that she had only been three steps up. Sara stood by the wall looking scared while Elizabeth knelt down and looked at Reggie's ankle. It was already swelling.

"I don't think anything's broken," she told the girl. "But I believe you need to let a doctor look at it."

Reggie groaned. "Oh, no."

"I'll call your mom." For once Elizabeth had remembered to put her cell phone in the pocket of her slacks. After assuring Linda that she didn't think anything was broken, she said she really did think it ought to be seen by a doctor.

Within five minutes Linda Tate was kneeling beside her daughter, with Chuck standing behind her. Finally she looked up at Elizabeth. "I agree we'd better have it looked at. The problem is getting her to the car."

With the garage under reconstruction, all the cars were at the Archer' parking lot and that was too far for Reggie to walk, even with help.

"I'll call an ambulance."

"Oh, no!" Reggie begged. "Please no ambulance!"

"Then how are we going to get you to the car?" her mother asked.

Elizabeth remembered the Archer's wagon and Mindy's wheelbarrow. They decided on the wheelbarrow with a blanket in it, so Elizabeth called Mindy who was there in less than ten minutes.

"I'm sorry it took me so long. I had to get it from the shed out back." She looked down at Reggie. "I'm so sorry you got hurt."

"I'll be fine." Reggie said, and looked at Sara, shaking her head. "Sorry."

Elizabeth placed a blanket that she'd gotten from the guest room and they all helped Reggie get in the wheelbarrow. Chuck insisted on pushing it ... and the adults allowed him to be the hero. But Linda and Elizabeth walked very close on each side with Mindy and Sara following.

When they had Reggie safely lying in the back seat of Linda's car, Elizabeth pulled out her cell phone. "I'll call the hospital and alert the ER that they will need to transport Reggie inside."

Chuck was up front in the passenger seat and there was no room for anybody else.

"Sara can stay with me," Elizabeth said. "And if she needs to go somewhere, I'll take her."

Linda smiled her thanks and started backing out of the parking space. She stopped and rolled down her window. "I forgot my cell phone. Would you call George?"

Elizabeth agreed and did so as soon as she phoned the hospital. Before they could start back to Tapestry Court, the door to the store opened and Jane Archer came running out.

"What happened? I saw you wheeling Reggie to the car but I was on the phone - business - and just got off."

They explained the situation and then Elizabeth introduced Sara to both Jane and Mindy.

"Is there anything I can do?" the store owner asked.

But there wasn't anything any of them could do so Jane went back inside and the others headed back toward Tapestry Court. Mindy said goodbye when they reached number five and disappeared behind the house with the wheelbarrow.

Elizabeth smiled at Sara. "I didn't ask if you wanted me to take you home now. We could have left when they did if you wanted. Are you ready to go?"

"Will I be in your way?" The girl's eyes pleaded with her to say 'no.'

"Of course not! I'd love to have you visit. I've never gotten to talk to you at rehearsals or on the drives home."

She saw the girl take a deep breath. *The child looks relieved.* Linda had told her the reason she drove her home was because her mother worked nights. *Probably tired of being alone all the time. It's summer, no school, not much to do.*

When they reached the kitchen, Elizabeth set the teapot on instead of heating water in the microwave. It would make it more special for her young guest who evidently liked old fashioned movies set in England.

"What kind of tea would you like, Sara? Regular or herbal?"

"What's the difference?"

"Regular tea has caffeine and tastes like the tea you'd get out at a restaurant, only hot. And herbal tea tastes like..." She looked at her tea shelf. "Blackberry or vanilla, rose hips, chamomile, black cherry, lemon, mandarin orange..."

Sara interrupted her. "I'd love to taste mandarin orange."

Elizabeth got down that box and set a teabag in each of her two new cups. This was the first time she'd used them since she bought them from a British specialty store in Lexington. The blue and white pattern was of English homes and the teacups were Windsor Castle.

"Mandarin Orange Spice is one of my favorites." She smiled at Sara. "I don't have any scones but I do have some apple pastries. Would you like one?"

"Yes, Ma'am." So Elizabeth pulled out two dessert plates with Dover Castle on them.

While the tea was brewing, Elizabeth asked Sara, "Do you mind if we pray for Reggie and also a prayer over our snack."

"No, Ma'am."

After Elizabeth prayed, they sat there in silence for a couple of minutes before Sara spoke.

"Reggie told me you're a psychiatrist or something?"

Elizabeth smiled at her. "No, that's a medical doctor. I'm a psychologist. I talk with people and try to help them work out their problems. I don't prescribe medications."

"Do people pay you to do that?" Sara looked so serious that Elizabeth immediately went into professional mode.

"Yes, when I'm working in my office. I'm on sabbatical now - away from my office business for a year. But I can still help people for free if I want to."

Sara eyes stared into hers. "Will you help me?" The stare was filled with both pain and hope.

"Of course I will, Sara. If I can."

***

In a month it would be over, finally, thank the gods!

Chapter Four

Ms. Drew really was a pretty lady. Chuck wasn't inter-ested in girls - or ladies - but he could see that all the oth-er guys noticed her. And watched her a lot. Well, Brandon Cress watched Ms. Taylor more than he did Ms. Drew, but he was the only one. And it was probably because she was the director. Mr. Cress was a cool dude. He mostly watched the boards and the stage. The lady and guys from New York had been there a week and the play would open in two weeks.

Chuck liked being on the stage crew but he would re-ally rather be working the technical stuff with Mr. Cress and the other guy from the theatre guild. His own boss, Mr. Lockland, could hardly pay attention to the set now that Ms. Drew was there. It was a good thing they'd had lots of weeks of practice before she came.

A run through of Act One was complete, and during the break Chuck headed to get an Ale-8-One from the snack table. Before he left the back stage area, he heard Mr. Cress and Mr. Lockland arguing.

"But he's having his gall bladder out and there's no way he'll be able to handle the lights."

"That's your problem," Mr. Lockland answered.

"I've already discussed it with Cal; he said to try the boy on sound and do the lights myself. He'll help you find somebody else to do props."

Chuck's heart leaped. He ducked back behind the curtain; he didn't want them to know he overheard, not when they were talking about him.

He really wanted that Ale-8-One but there was no way to get to the snack table without passing them. Unless he went the other direction, around the back of the stage.

He heard Ms. Drew's voice, sounding softer than usual and almost like she was pleading. "Come on, pretty please! You can hang in there a little longer. Remember how much it's worth."

He was surprised to hear the voice of Albert Shaw, the other guy from New York, who was playing the Wizard. "All right. But I'll be glad to get out of this ... this den of goodness!"

Ms. Drew laughed.

Chuck hurried past the area where the two were hidden by curtains and onward toward the table of food and drinks. As soon as he passed them, he ran into Ms. Coulter and since she had her Tin Man costume on, it hurt his head. But she was a teacher so he didn't say anything except, "Scuse me", as he went onward, rubbing the new bump. There sure better be some Ale-8-One left on that table.

And there was! Just one and Chuck grabbed it as soon as he saw it, even though there was no one else in sight, much less in reach of the bottle.

***

Elizabeth was very glad that Reggie's fall had only resulted in a strain instead of a sprain or break. A few days in a bandage and it was as good as new. But she was still worried about the girl's crush on the handsome youth pastor. And glad that they were in the last few weeks of the play. When it was over, Reggie would be removed from the - danger? But what could be dangerous? The man was obviously a wonderful Christian and Elizabeth had watched to make sure he handled Reggie's flirtations the right way. And there was no question about Reggie flirting. It was embarrassingly obvious. Elizabeth was surprised that Linda hadn't mentioned it.

She'd been helping Linda a lot in the daytime while Galen was at work. And she'd even gone to rehearsals several nights when he was going to be late, or bringing work to do at home. It was those times when she noticed the escalation of Reggie's crush.

It was the opposite of what anyone would have expected, except Elizabeth. Sara Conley who, according to the girl herself, had a bad reputation, didn't flirt with anyone. Elizabeth was growing very fond of Sara. She sat with Elizabeth whenever they were both there at rehearsals. And it was interesting that she seemed more interested in Elizabeth than in the New York actress who seemed to claim everyone else's attention. Elizabeth smiled at her own pride in the thought. But then the pain hit her when she thought back on Sara's confession.

~ ~ ~

"It's so embarrassing." Sara's eyes had filled with tears as she looked away from Elizabeth. Elizabeth immediately got up and grabbed a box of tissues from the counter and brought them to the table. The girl breathed a deep sigh as she took one and wiped the tears away.

"Sara, I've heard everything there is to hear. Nothing shocks or embarrasses me." She smiled reassuringly.

Sara nodded. "It was when I was twelve and my mom... well she had a man over to the apartment and she passed out. He came upstairs to my bedroom." She bit her lip. "I didn't know what to say. So I didn't say anything. He, uh, he got in bed with me. And he, uh, he started trying to kiss me. I didn't know what to do but I hated it. I pushed him away. And then he said..."

The tears came again and she took another tissue. "He said, 'Come on. Don't act prissy with me. You're your mother's daughter, ain't you? You'll like it.' But I jumped out of the bed and when he tried to pull me back I bit him on the arm."

Elizabeth couldn't stop the laughter and Sara looked surprised.

"Good for you!"

The girl smiled weakly. "That was okay?"

Elizabeth nodded. "Absolutely."

Sara took a deep breath. "I left my bedroom and went downstairs. He followed me, but he didn't bother me anymore. He just left, and slammed the door behind him. I never told my mom."

"Why? Why didn't you tell your mother?"

Sara bit her lip. "I ... I'm not sure. I think because she might have gotten mad at me cause he was her boyfriend."

"But, honey, you didn't do anything to cause him to act like that."

The tears swelled up again. "But he said I was my mother's daughter. He meant I was just like her." Then the lips pursed and anger filled her eyes. "I don't want to be like her, Mrs. Delaney. I don't!!! But the kids at school act like I am that way too."

"I don't think you're like that, Sara. And neither does the Tate family. We all think you are a very nice girl." Elizabeth reached over and took Sara's hand.

"And you need to know something. What happened to you has happened to many, many girls. And all of them didn't handle it in as grown up a way as you did. You've got something very special inside you, a goodness that God gave you. And no one can take that away."

For the first time ever, Elizabeth saw a look of joy on Sara's face. "I'm good inside? Not bad?"

Elizabeth laughed gently. "It seems that way to me. Do you know the Lord?"

Sara nodded. "Yes, I heard about him on TV and asked Jesus into my heart. And now I go to the Baptist youth group. That's where I heard about the play, from Reverend Sutton."

Elizabeth stood up went over to hug Sara. She held her close to her own heart. "Then we're family, aren't we?"

Sara drew back in surprise and stared into Elizabeth's face. "We are?"

"Yes, we are in the family of God. Family forever."

Sara initiated the hug this time. "Thank you. Thank you so much!"

~~~

Elizabeth felt as much gratitude at the relationship as Sara had expressed.

She was also surprised but glad at the friendship that was developing between Galen and Harold Fowler too. Ever since the night they were invited to supper there, the two men seemed to grow closer, and one night when Elizabeth got home from rehearsal, she'd been shocked to find them on her patio sharing coffee.

She and Galen had never mentioned having a child again. And he seemed to have forgotten it was ever an issue.

But she couldn't forget.

***

"This costume is NOT acceptable!" The strident voice cut across the low murmur of giggles and exclamations as the cast reacted to the distribution of their apparel for the play. Complete silence followed the remark and all eyes turned to Carolyn Simpson Brock who stood holding up Dorothy's outfit for all to see. Her daughter stood beside her looking at the floor.

Elizabeth's heart tightened when she saw the look on Margaret's face. Humiliation and embarrassment were written all over her. *Poor child. How awful to have such a pushy mother.*

Linda Tate emerged from a sea of Monkeys and Munchkins and went over to the Brocks. She had the Munchkin parents bring their children's costumes at the same time as the rest of the cast would get their rentals so that no one would feel left out at any time.

"What's wrong?" Linda's voice was pleasant and there was no hint of the irritation that Elizabeth knew was simmering inside her friend in reaction to Carolyn Brock.

"Look at this!" Carolyn pointed to the gingham dress. "It's faded. It looks like the dress of a...a ragamuffin."

Linda took the dress and examined it closely. "I can't see any tears or anything wrong. Actually I think that it's not faded, that's just the shade of this material."

Carolyn's eyes narrowed. "Well, whatever the reason, it's not acceptable!"

Linda answered her calmly but Elizabeth could see that her hands were tightly gripping the costume. "What would you suggest that we do, since the play is just a week away? We don't have time to send to another outlet for a different costume."

"I would suggest that you get busy and make one that is suitable. I notice that your own daughter has a very lovely and bright costume." Carolyn's tone of voice was syrupy sweet.

Linda didn't say anything for a few seconds. Elizabeth saw her swallow hard before she responded.

"All right, Carolyn, I will do that but you need to go pick out the pattern and material yourself. If you will phone me at my home when you have them, we'll make a time for you to bring them and Margaret there. But you better get them tomorrow in order for me to have enough time to complete it before dress rehearsal next week." Linda stooped and picked up the Ruby Slippers and the brown tieups. "Do the shoes suit you?"

Carolyn looked at them and nodded.

"Well then, that's taken care of." Linda returned to the other children, and the low murmur of voices and giggles resumed.

Elizabeth looked once again at Margaret whose eyes were now spilling over with tears. Her mother looked at her and frowned. Then she leaned down and whispered something in the child's ear.

Margaret went toward the rest room and Carolyn began folding the offending costume and replacing it in the box.

Elizabeth quietly slipped toward the ladies room. Inside she saw Margaret Brock standing against the wall holding her face in her hands with her shoulders heaving.

Elizabeth went to her. "There now. It'll be all right."

Margaret's arms went around her waist and she held the child close.

"No, it won't. It won't ever be all right. She makes everybody hate me."

"I don't think everybody hates you." Elizabeth made her voice to be as soothing as possible. Then she laughed. "I don't hate you, Margaret. I think you are a very nice girl. Pretty. Talented. And I mean it, you are very nice." She cast her mind back over the previous weeks.

"Why, I remember the time you gave the last cookie to the little boy who plays Toto. I know he doesn't hate you!"

"I need to get some toilet paper." Margaret pulled away and reached into the stall, retrieved the paper, and blew her nose.

Elizabeth went on talking. "And I know Reggie Tate likes you. I ride with them all the time and she talked about how you are a lot of fun to work with."

Margaret's face brightened. "Really?"

Elizabeth could tell by the look that Margaret looked up to Reggie.

"Yes, Reggie thinks you are a lot of fun. And all the adults I've heard are very impressed with your talent and your respect for them." *I won't tell you what they say about your mother!*

Margaret looked up with such sadness in her eyes that Elizabeth wanted to hug her again.

"Thank you. Mostly it's the kids my age that hate me. My mother is always acting like I am better than they are.

Every time I think I have a friend, she makes them mad and they never come around again."

Elizabeth wasn't going to pretend she thought the child was exaggerating. "I'm sorry."

Margaret's little chest rose and fell with a big sigh.

She seems relieved. Could it be that this is the first time she has talked about this with another person?

Elizabeth pulled a paper towel out of the holder and held it under the faucet. She handed it to Margaret. "Here, wash your face and you'll feel better."

The girl did as she was told and grabbed another towel to dry her face. She looked anxiously in the mirror. "Can you tell I've been crying?"

Elizabeth studied her face and then nodded. "Well, maybe just a tiny cry."

Margaret smiled.

On the drive home, Elizabeth complemented her friend. "You were really good with Carolyn Brock. I was impressed."

Linda shook her head. "It wasn't easy. I wanted to... well, I wanted to be unchristian and unladylike."

Elizabeth laughed. "I don't blame you."

Reggie's voice came from the back seat. "I felt so sorry for Dorothy, I mean Margaret. She looked like she wanted to die of embarrassment."

Elizabeth didn't want to betray Margaret's trust but she did want Reggie to know that she could probably help the child.

"You know, Margaret really thinks a lot of you, Reggie. I wish you could spend more time with her. I think it would help her. I don't think she has a very happy life."

"Who could? With that woman as a mother?"

Linda laughed. "So does this mean that your own mother isn't so bad?"

"Mom! You know you could never be like Mrs. Brock!"

"Well, you know they will probably be coming over tomorrow afternoon to bring the pattern and let me fit it on Margaret. So we're going to have to pray for patience and kindness."

"Maybe we could invite Margaret for a sleepover."

Elizabeth smiled and turned toward the back seat. "That's a great idea, Reggie. I think it would do Margaret a world of good."

Linda said, "It's okay with me. When Carolyn calls, I'll ask her."

They pulled into the now parking lot at the Ames' store. Linda turned to Reggie. "Would you like to invite Sara too?"

Reggie hesitated for a few seconds. "No. Not at the same time as Margaret. Sara and I would probably talk about high school stuff and make her feel left out. I would like to have Sara over again sometime though."

Elizabeth's admiration for the teen grew again. *How perceptive and kind.*

***

Margaret Brock was a perfect guest. Linda thought she was the most polite child she ever met. She seemed interested in every member of the family.

She won Chuck's respect by acting fascinated by his pet hamster. And even Linda who was not interested in hamsters or paid any attention to it had to admit that it was funny when the tiny animal did back flips if the running wheel was removed from his cage.

George was also charmed by her during dinner as she asked him, in a very serious and interested tone of voice, how many different kinds of businesses were owned by Tapestry Industries.

She and Reggie helped Linda clear the table and load the dishwasher.

"Mom, is it okay if I show Margaret the park and if we go to Ms. Dailey's – uh – Mrs. Delaney's?"

"It's fine for you to show her the park but let me call Elizabeth first."

When Elizabeth agreed that it was okay for them to visit, Linda hung up the phone and watched the two girls leave by the kitchen door.

Reggie was saying, "This is the neatest house that the Delaney's live in. It belonged to my grandfather and we rent it to them."

***

Elizabeth smiled when she opened the door to find Reggie and the Brock child standing there.

"Reggie, Margaret! Come in!"

"I hope you don't mind if we came over. Do you? Mind, I mean? Is it okay?"

Elizabeth laughed. "Yes, it's okay. I told your mother. My husband is in the library catching up on some business so he can forget about it and relax this weekend. So I'm not busy right now. What are you girls up to?"

"I wanted to show Margaret your house. And the garden. Is it okay?"

"Of course. We'll just skip the library this time."

Elizabeth started up the stairs and then stopped. "Tell you what, Reggie. You know where everything is. Why don't you show Margaret yourself and come join me in the kitchen when you're through. I did this experiment today with a new cheesecake recipe and you're welcome to try it out if you like."

She turned back. "And be careful coming down those steps!"

"No worry!" Reggie laughed and as the two disappeared to the upper floor, Elizabeth heard her telling the younger girl that this was the place of the accident that caused the strained ankle that kept her in an ankle bandage for several days.

When they joined her, both girls declined cheesecake but said they would like a cup of tea and a cookie.

When the three were seated around the table, Elizabeth asked how the Dorothy costume was coming.

"Mom hasn't started on it yet. Well, I think that's what she's doing now."

"It's going to be pretty," Margaret said.

"Have you ever been in a play before, Margaret?"

The girl shook her head. "No, never. But when Mother saw that it was the Wizard of Oz, she said that I was the perfect age for Dorothy and should try out." She paused a minute. "I really didn't want to do it but now I like it. A lot. It's fun. And it feels important to work with real actors from New York. Even if one of them is just from here... and a cousin."

Elizabeth was startled. "Cousin? I didn't know that."

"Ms. Drew and my Mother are third cousins or something like that. But I don't think they know each other very well. They don't act like they are friends or related or anything."

Elizabeth nodded. "I've never seen them talking. But now that you mention it, there is a resemblance between them. Both very attractive ladies." She smiled at Margaret. "Just like you're going to be.

Reggie pushed back her chair. "I guess we better be going. Thank you for letting us see the house."

"And for the tea and cookies," Margaret added.

***

Reggie stared at her reflection in the mirror. With her hair pulled up, did she look older? She only had two more weeks to get David's attention. The thought almost made her panic. She just knew he was the one for her. God's plan. Maybe Mom and Dad would let her change youth groups. But she knew that was wishful thinking. They were Methodists through and through.

She dropped her hair back down. No, nothing made her look older. It was going to take God working a miracle.

When they got to rehearsal that night, she was surprised to see David Sutton with a strange woman. A pretty woman. Blonde, with a good figure. And she and David were staring at each other. In a sickening way.

Then the woman sat quietly and watched while David became the Tin Man. Reggie wasn't as thrilled as usual with the time she got to interact with the four main characters. It wasn't quite the same with the blonde lady there. Glinda the Good didn't seem quite as glamorous tonight.

The big surprise came after the rehearsal was over. Glenda Taylor had set up a table in the hallway and there were bottles of fake champagne and plastic champagne glasses. It was Brandon Cress who made the announcement.

"We are so proud and happy to announce the happy news that our own David Sutton and this beautiful lady, Amber Knight, are engaged to be married." He turned to David. "When is the wedding?"

David grinned as he hugged the blonde lady. "The first week in December. And you all are invited!"

Brandon then popped the cork on the first bottle of fake champagne, while Glenda opened the others. They poured out glassfuls for everyone, and Brandon made a toast.

Reggie didn't hear the words of the toast because there was such a buzzing in her ears. And she felt like she was going to throw up.

***

Nobody suspects anything. Everything is all fun and games, laughter and excitement. Just the way it should be. For now.

Chapter Five

Excitement reigned in the Simpsonton High School auditorium. Opening night was here and in only a few minutes the curtain would go up on Act One, Scene One.

Reggie's heart beat hard in anticipation of her own entrance but she watched with pride as Dorothy and Toto tried to escape the tornado and ended up in the land of Oz on top of the Wicked Witch of the East.

She could see Carolyn Brock on the first row watching anxiously. *I hope she tells Margaret what a good job she does.*

Then it was her turn. She was surprised at how natural it felt to be Glinda the Good. It wasn't scary at all, even with hundreds of people watching. When she left the stage, she was sorry her next scene wasn't 'til near the end of the show.

She was also surprised at how quickly she'd gotten over her fascination with Pastor Sutton. No more foolishness about thinking of him as David. How could she have been so stupid?

She was sorry she couldn't stand in the wings and watch Sara and the other munchkins, or Margaret as Dorothy. But she had to go to the girl's dressing room...well, it was really the band room when school was going on.

Sara came in shortly and the two, who were older than the other girls, went off to sit alone. Sara asked, "Okay?"

Reggie knew she meant about Pastor Sutton. She wished now she'd never told about her silly crush. But at least she only told Sara. Nobody else knew. "I'm fine."

And when Sara looked at her questioningly, she said, "Really. Completely over it!"

And her friend smiled.

***

Harold and Lucy went to all four performances. It was exciting having their own niece and nephew involved in a show. It was almost like having grandchildren who lived close by.

Harold was glad Reggie got the part she wanted but he wished it was bigger. She was certainly the most beautiful actress on the stage, Hanley Drew notwithstanding. And young Chuck was bursting with pride over being the sound technician. It had been a late appointment for the boy but he was a quick learner and did a perfect job.

Harold liked watching the crowds at the end of the show. They waited patiently in line to shake hands with the performers and tell them what a good job they did. And he noticed how Hanley Drew graciously accepted each complement as though it was an everyday event. And he guessed that, for her, it was. He'd noticed that by the time the cast took their bow, the green makeup was gone. He guessed she wanted that pretty face seen there, and especially in the greeting line.

***

Galen waited until Saturday night before attending the show. He would certainly be glad when it was over and Elizabeth back to normal. The past two weeks had not been fun. When he came home after a long day's work and the drive from Lexington, Elizabeth barely had time to kiss him on the cheek and point him to a plate in the microwave before running off to a rehearsal or, on the last two nights, a performance. But after tomorrow afternoon his happy married life could resume.

He was surprised to find that the play was not as boring as he thought it would be. The music was excellent and the kids were cute. He supposed that it was the cute kids that put the longing for motherhood in Elizabeth. That had really shocked him. He thought they were old enough not to have to even discuss the children thing. He was glad when she finally dropped it. He did not want to have to go into his reasons for not wanting children.

***

The final curtain call of the final performance was beginning that Sunday afternoon, and Hanley Drew was nowhere to be seen. Ron Lockland motioned to Elizabeth to join him there at the edge of the stage and then whispered.

"Would you go get Hanley? She's going to miss her bow if she doesn't hurry."

Elizabeth knocked on the door of the room that had been set aside for the actress but there was no answer. She opened it cautiously and peered inside.

The body was slumped over the dressing table and only the pool of blood beneath her chair was an indication that she was not just resting.

"Hanley!" Elizabeth knew by the amount of blood that it was useless to call her name but she couldn't help herself. When there was no answer, she pulled her cell phone out of her pocket with shaking fingers, turned it on, and punched in 911.

"I am Elizabeth Daily of Tapestry Court," she reported in a calm voice, much calmer than she felt. "I am back stage at the high school and came to get Hanley Drew for the curtain call. I found her sitting with a pool of blood at her feet and she doesn't appear to be alive. I didn't touch her because I thought you wouldn't want me to. Can someone come?"

The dispatcher assured her that a squad car with officers would be sent immediately.

"Could you tell them to come to the back entrance, where the band room is? So people won't get upset."

The answer came quickly. "Ma'am if this is a murder, they will want to secure the place and interview people."

"Of course. Thank you." Elizabeth ended the call but didn't turn the phone off.

She closed the door to the dressing room and went out to the wings again. "Hanley can't come for curtain call," she said to Ron Lockland.

He frowned. "Is something wrong?"

Elizabeth nodded. Suddenly her knees gave way and she caught herself before she fell.

"Are you okay?" The stage manager was looking out at the bowing cast.

Elizabeth suddenly sat down on a stool there beside the curtain rope.

"No. I'm not okay."

Ron looked at her with more attention than previously.

"I'm so sorry." She knew the man was in love with Hanley Drew. "It's Hanley. She's dead."

"What?" Ron started back toward the dressing room.

Elizabeth jumped up and ran after him. She caught him by the arm just as he reached the door. "Don't! Don't touch anything. The police are on their way."

He stopped still. "What?" His pale face looked even whiter than usual in the dim lighting of the back hallway.

"There is a lot of blood. A whole pool of it, right under her chair." She repeated her earlier statement. "I'm so sorry."

She could hear the audience applause from the front of the theatre. It was strange to hear that while looking at a man drained of all signs of life in his facial expression.

She shook her head. "I'm just so sorry."

"Why blood? How?" He stared at her. "How did she die?"

"I don't know. I didn't touch her. I called the police."
Just then they heard the sirens.

***

The shocked cast was gathered in the band room, awaiting the police detective. The squad car had arrived in time to quarantine the entire theatre audience, at least those who had not left before the curtain call, if any.

Elizabeth realized that more than likely if the killer was a member of the audience, they would have left after committing the crime. She was sure the police realized that too but they made the announcement that no one would be allowed to leave before they left their names and contact information.

Two officers commandeered the table that was set up earlier in the hallway for ticket sales, and they were taking down information when the chief of police announced that the cast and crew should all assemble in the band room.

Ron and Lisa sat apart from the others. They were holding hands. It was a visual statement of the special relationship they shared with Hanley Drew of which the others were not a part. Elizabeth was sorry for them. They both looked devastated.

When the police entered the room, they took the names of the small children and their parents and then dismissed them before turning to the rest of the cast and crew.

"I am Detective Joseph Reardon. We will need a statement from each of you as to your movements during the time that Ms. Drew left the stage until the discovery of her body. Are there those of you who were on stage in plain view the entire time?"

Ron Lockland withdrew his hand from Lisa's and stood up slowly. Elizabeth thought he looked like he had aged twenty years.

"I can give you that information." He pulled his script from his back pocket. "Actually no, there is not one actor who was in view on stage the entire time...most of the time, yes. But not the whole time." He turned to Cal Morgan. "What about your crew?"

Cal looked at Brandon Cress, who immediately nodded.

"There were two of us in the sound and light booth. Chuck Tate and I never left after intermission." He pointed to the boy.

Detective Reardon looked at Chuck. "Is that right?" He nodded. "Neither of you went to the bathroom or anything?" He shook his head.

The detective nodded in satisfaction. "Okay that eliminates you. You can go now."

Chuck stood up. "Sir, can I stay with my mom and sister?" He pointed to Linda and Reggie.

"Okay, we'll start with you two." He got the names and addresses of the family and the times of the movements of Glinda the Good. He questioned Linda extensively about her whereabouts backstage during the crucial time but she said she had already helped everyone into all the costumes and stood in the wings watching the end of the last performance.

Elizabeth raised her hand. "Officer I can attest to that. I was watching with her until time for the curtain call and then I was asked to go get Ms. Drew when she wasn't there to take her bow."

The Detective looked at his notes. "You are Elizabeth Daily? The one who called us?"

Elizabeth could feel herself blushing. "I'm sorry. Yes, that's me but I'm now Elizabeth Delaney." She saw his questioning look. "I've only been married a few months and I was so shocked when I found Ms. Drew, I guess I just ..." she shrugged.

The officer nodded, made a notation in his book, and then dismissed the Tate family. Linda came over to Elizabeth and whispered. "You rode with us! How will you get home?"

"I knew I'd be one of the last to be let go since I found the body. I've already called Galen and alerted him. I told him I'd call when I needed him to come and get me."

Linda looked at her more closely. "I think you should call and ask him to come now."

Elizabeth nodded. "I think you are right." And with trembling fingers, she picked up her cell phone.

While she waited to be questioned again, she thought over the past few weeks. Was there anything that indicated this was going to happen? If so, she couldn't remember it. Then an unpleasant thought struck her. *Except that Glenda Taylor looked unhappy with the way Hanley flirted with Brandon Cress. Of course Hanley flirted with everybody. Surely there wasn't anything special there.*

Elizabeth liked the librarian and didn't want to think of her as a suspect in a murder case. But who else? *Ron Lockland obviously adores her...adored her.*

Another thought sprang up and made her heart feel lighter. *We know nothing about the two men from New York. They could have motives that we know nothing about.*

She really hoped the killer wasn't someone from Simpsonton.

She watched Detective Reardon as he talked to those cast members remaining. Cal Morgan and Albert Shaw sat on the back row of chairs apart from the others. They both had grim expressions and she wondered if they knew that they would probably be the favorite suspects.

A knock came on the door and then Galen stuck his head inside. The police Detective stopped and turned to him. "Yes? May I help you?"

Galen pointed to her. "I came to be with my wife." He didn't wait for permission but came over and sat in the chair beside her which had been vacated by Linda Tate.

The chief looked like he might object but gave a slight shrug of his shoulders and turned back to Glenda Taylor.

Galen put his arm around her and drew her close to him. "Okay, Bits?"

She nodded, not trusting herself to speak. A lump had come to her throat when she saw him in the doorway. They sat there in silence and waited her turn.

Finally there were only six people left in the room – Elizabeth and Galen, Cal Morgan and Albert Shaw, Ron Lockland and the detective.

Reardon looked at Galen through narrowed eyes. "You weren't here?"

"No sir. My wife called me when the people she rode with were dismissed."

"Where were you during the play?"

"At home...#1 Tapestry Court."

"Any witnesses to that?"

Galen looked surprised. "No, sir. Just me."

Elizabeth was surprised too. *Is he thinking that he is a criminal who returns to the scene of the crime or something?*

She interrupted. "Detective Reardon, my husband came to the play last night. He had no reason to be here today."

Reardon looked skeptical but dropped it. He turned to the two men from New York.

"Hanley Drew was a friend of yours?"

Both men nodded.

"Must have been a close friend to get you to come all the way here for three weeks."

Cal Morgan shrugged. "Close enough."

"Did you have a romantic relationship with her?"

"No, just friendship." Cal shook his head.

"And you?" The officer looked at Albert Shaw.

He giggled. "You've got to be kidding. Look at me."

Detective Reardon repeated his question. "Did you have a romantic relationship with her?"

"No, I didn't."

"What did she pay you to come for this three week period?"

Elizabeth was surprised by the question. It never occurred to her that Hanley might have paid the men.

Cal Morgan looked over at Ron Lockland before he answered. "Two thousand apiece."

"And did she ask you to act like you were her boyfriend?"

Cal looked at the floor, and nodded.

Ron was looking at Cal with complete disgust.

Reardon turned back to Albert Shaw. "And your part in all this?"

He looked sullen. "I just came to be the Wizard."

But Elizabeth saw the look he gave Cal. There was something the two men were hiding. She remembered Linda's first reaction to Albert.

Cal spoke up. "You can't really think we had anything to do with Hanley's death. Who would kill the goose that lays the golden eggs?"

The Policeman looked at Cal Morgan with narrowed eyes, and then nodded slowly. "I'm assuming you two were planning on returning to New York soon?"

"Tomorrow morning. We have airline reservations...us and Hanley."

"I'm afraid I'm going to have to ask you to stay over. If there's a problem with the tickets, the feds will make sure it's taken care of."

"You mean we have to stay? Here?" Albert Shaw's voice held complete disgust.

Cal reached over and touched his arm. "It's okay, Al." He turned back to the officer. "How long do you think it will be?"

"Just a few days, 'til the state and federal guys get here and talk to you."

Cal nodded. "I guess we'll stay at the same place. Loury's. We're there for tonight. If they don't have room Monday and Tuesday nights, I'll let you know."

"Do you have cell phones?"

"Yes."

"Did you give your address and phone numbers to the officer earlier?"

"Yes."

"Okay then. That's all for now. How are you getting back and forth?"

"I guess Lisa Coulter will still transport us. But maybe we should rent a car. She'll be pretty upset. Is there someplace here in town?"

"Just one and I doubt if they'll be open on Sunday night."

"Well, thank you. We'll figure something out. You'll let us know when we're needed again?"

When the actors from New York had gone, Reardon looked over at Ron Lockland. "You are the stage manager?"

Lockland nodded but didn't say anything.

"Tell me about the timing here. How much time elapsed from the time Ms. Drew was on stage until the curtain call?"

Ron looked over at Elizabeth. Her heart ached for him. It was obvious he was so devastated that he couldn't think straight.

"Sir," she got the officer's attention. "Mr. Lockland is in a state of shock. He and Ms. Drew were old friends. But I think I can answer your question. It was approximately fifteen minutes." She hoped that was right. The wicked witch was melted and then Dorothy and the trio returned to Oz, the Wizard took off in the balloon without her, Glinda the Good came and told her how to get home, she got home to Aunt Em and the others and the play ended. But she added, "I think Mr. Lockland can give you a more accurate time later, after he's had time to think it through and look at the script."

The policeman let Ron Lockland go and turned his attention to Elizabeth. But he seemed to relax.

After all, he knows I have an alibi. I was with Linda Tate during the time Hanley was killed.

But the Detective did not seem to know that. "I'm sure you are distressed Mrs..." He looked at the paper in his hand. "Mrs. Delaney, but you must realize that we have to examine the possibility that you stabbed Hanley Drew when you were sent to get her."

Elizabeth was startled. "I hadn't realized that. But I see what you mean."

Galen's arm tightened around her shoulder. "Now, look here..."

"It's okay, Galen. He's just doing his job." She turned back to the detective. "Of course if she was okay, she would have shown up for curtain call. After all she was an actress."

Reardon nodded. "There is that."

He finally let them leave. After making sure they would be available for further questioning if necessary.

The telephone rang later that night and startled Elizabeth from her musings on the happenings of the day. It was still hard to believe that Hanley Drew had been murdered right here at the Simpsonton High School during their performance.

She was surprised when the voice on the other end introduced himself as Deputy Collins of the county sheriff's office. She liked the man, rough around the edges though he was, when she encountered him several months earlier during her investigations into Colonel Tapestry's past.

"Well, hello, Deputy Collins. How are you?"

"Just fine, Ma'am. And yourself?"

"I am fine too."

"What I'm calling about is this murder that happened this afternoon. I hear you found the body?"

"Yes, I did. It was horrible."

"Do you know who did it?"

"I have no idea."

"A buddy of mine was talking 'bout it and told me you found 'er. I told him you are as good a detective as anybody I know."

"Well, thank you, Deputy."

"I meant it. I guess it's natural – you knowin' 'bout people's minds – bein' a shrink and all."

Elizabeth didn't bother to suppress her amusement, since he couldn't see her over the phone.

"Yes, I guess you're right."

"I told him they ought to get you in on it. Now I didn't tell 'em 'bout the Colonel and all – you said that was a secret and I don't tell no secrets trusted to me."

"Thank you, Deputy."

"Anyhow, my friend said the police department couldn't get no amateur involved; they have to work with the State Police and the FBI."

"Right."

"But I said I bet you'd figure it out first. So I thought I'd call and tell you."

"Thank you, Deputy. I appreciate your confidence."

"And if I win, I'll split with you."

Huh? "Uh, I don't know exactly what you mean, Deputy Collins."

"Me and my friend. We made a bet. He bet the state or feds would figure it out first and I bet you would. So I wanted you to know. And, like I said, I'll split. So your part will be $250."

Elizabeth was speechless.

***

The cast party was cancelled but Sara was invited to come to Reggie's house even though Reggie was leaving for camp the next day. Reggie's mom said she didn't like to send Sara home alone after the horrible happening of the day.

"I just can't believe it," Sara said for the sixth time.

Reggie shook her head. "Me either. Who could have done it?" She thought a minute. "But we should be able to figure it out. Or at least eliminate some people like they do in books."

"What do you mean?"

"Oh, you know. Okay, Ms. Drew was on stage and then she left and went to her dressing room. Somebody had to go there and kill her before the end of the show. Who could it have been?"

Sara thought a minute. "It wasn't us Munchkins or you. We were all together, on stage while we told the Wizard and Dorothy good-bye and then back at the band room til they called us for the curtain call."

Reggie grinned. "I really didn't think it was any of us kids."

Sara seemed to be completely in detective mode and ignored her. "And it couldn't have been any of the stage crew because there are three scene changes right in a row and if anybody had been absent, the others would have noticed."

Reggie nodded. "You're right."

Sara continued, "So that leaves the last scene. We can count out Dorothy and Toto and Auntie Em and the uncle and farm hands. It couldn't have been them. There wouldn't be time, would there?"

"I'm not sure." Reggie shook her head. "But if so, who does that leave?"

Sara counted off on her fingers. "The Wizard, the Scarecrow, the Tin Man, the Cowardly Lion. Anybody else?"

***

Everything went perfectly. And the perfect person would be blamed. As long as nobody saw anything. But what if...

Chapter Six

Elizabeth was grateful that Galen called the bank that Monday morning and took the day off. She didn't like being alone after the shock of the previous afternoon and she was glad he was here to track down the reason behind the silence in the Court.

Not that the silence wasn't welcome on this unhappy Monday morning but why was it there? It had been there too often; the garage should have been finished a month ago. Galen called George to find out.

When he hung up the house phone on the kitchen wall, he turned to her.

"George said he was just getting ready to call you. He'd already called Linda and Harold. It seems that a couple of the carpenters were in a wreck Saturday night and the contractor phoned to tell him they'll be okay but it will probably be a couple of weeks before they can start back on the job."

Elizabeth could hear the shrillness in her own voice. "But that leaves us open for ... how much longer? Another month? They've already taken weeks longer than we thought it would. Workmen these days are so unreliable."

Galen walked over and bent down to hug her. "I'm sorry."

Immediately Elizabeth felt ashamed. What was wrong with her these days? The first thought that came to her mind should have been to pray for the injured workmen. She looked up at Galen.

"No, I'm sorry. I really hope the men aren't hurt badly. I don't know what's wrong with me."

"Well, you found a dead body in a pool of blood yesterday. Don't you think that might cause a little bit of shock? Even to a psychologist?"

She felt her muscles relax. And she gave a short laugh. "Yes, I guess it would." She leaned her head back against his chest.

"And Bits, I've been talking to Harold. He's convinced me that I shouldn't have reacted the way I did when you mentioned us, uh, having a baby."

Elizabeth felt a thrill go through her. "Do you mean you've changed your mind?"

Immediately Galen drew away from her and went over to the coffee pot. She watched as he poured himself a fresh cup. Then he came back to the table and sat down.

"No. Definitely not. But I shouldn't have gotten angry. I should be flattered that you wanted to have my child. I admit it was a shock. But to accuse you of going through a menopause thing... Well, will you forgive me?"

She was disappointed but forced a smile to her face. "Of course." When she reached across the table, he took her hand and they smiled at each other.

When he finished his coffee, he got up from the table. "I think I'll go work from the computer for a while if that's okay with you."

She nodded. "Maybe I should go do some work myself. I'll call Mindy and see if she's busy."

A few minutes later, she stuck her head in the upstairs room Galen was now using as an office. "Mindy's free now. I think I'll run down there."

Galen just nodded.

On the way to Number Five, she was glad to see Jenny Anderson out in the front yard of Number Three. She hadn't seen the young wife all summer.

"Hi, stranger!"

Jenny looked up from the rose bush she was carefully trimming, and smiled. "Hi, Elizabeth! Long time, no see." Then the smile left. "I heard about the ... the tragedy yesterday. I'm so sorry."

Elizabeth stopped. "Yes, it was awful. Had you met Hanley Drew?"

"No, we never even made it to the play. I felt bad because of the Tates. We really should have gone. But Joel asked me to go to a sales conference with him in Gatlinburg, Tennessee, and I'm not sorry that we went. We left Thursday morning and just got back last night. The Conference was Friday night and Saturday, so we got to spend some just fun time."

"That's wonderful, Jenny. What tourist stuff did you do?"

The younger woman's face lit up. "The Titanic Museum! Joel surprised me as soon as we checked into the hotel. He wouldn't tell me where we were going til we were there. It was wonderful! They even had a special room dedicated to the movie."

Elizabeth knew that Jenny Anderson was an avid movie buff and that would have been a special event for her. How clever of Joel to take her there. She was so happy to have played a part in helping the couple's marriage grow healthier.

"And we stayed at the Inn at Christmas Place! That's where the convention was held. It's really neat! Christmas decorations everywhere and a clock..." Dismay came over the pretty young face. "I'm sorry. Here I am going on and on about my trip when such an awful thing has happened here in Simpsonton."

"No," Elizabeth protested. "I'm thrilled to hear your good news."

"So what happened? The news reports didn't tell us much, just that the famous Broadway actress was found dead, presumed murdered, in her dressing room after the play."

Elizabeth grimaced. "I was the one who found her. So I was the first suspect."

Shock flooded Jenny's face. "I'm so sorry! I had no idea. I mean, I knew you were helping with the play and so would have met her. But..."

"It wasn't pleasant. But really the police have no clue as far as I know. State and federal agents are being called in. I hope they find something soon. It's... well, it's unsettling to know it must be somebody that we worked with."

"I can imagine." Jenny shook her head. "I hope with you. That they settle it soon."

Elizabeth walked on, resisting the impulse to cross the walk and visit with Linda. Mindy was expecting her.

***

Reggie hung up the phone and turned to her mother.

"Sara had forgotten I'm leaving for camp today. She wanted me to go to the movie tonight. A girl in our class called her and she's going but was hoping I'd go too. You know, I'm going to miss Sara. It was neat having a real friend, and seeing her almost every day."

They'd just gotten back from taking Sara home and picking up a few last minute things from the store before leaving for camp.

Linda nodded. "Sara is a nice girl. When you get back next week, you can have her over." She shook her head. "It's obvious her mother doesn't mind her being away from home."

"Mom, isn't that awful? How could a mother be like that?"

Linda shook her head. "I don't know, Sweetie. I honestly don't know. But we don't know what kind of home

Sara's mother was raised in. That's why we aren't supposed to judge."

"Not judge!" Reggie glared. "Not judge the way she
treats her kid, and ignores her, and doesn't take care of
her?"

"Well, of course we judge that her behavior is not good,
but we also have to remember that Jesus forgives. And we
are supposed to forgive too."

Reggie glared at her Mother. "How do you forgive and
forget when it goes on all the time?"

Linda shook her head. "I don't know. We really need to
pray. For both Sara and her mother." She put the last dish
away in the cabinet. "Well are you ready to leave?"

"I guess so." She'd really been looking forward to camp
but now...

"Do you want me to call and cancel?" Mom sounded
like she'd be really glad to do that. And it was tempting.

She shook her head. "No, I probably need to go."

Her mom smiled. "Yes, I'm a little jealous. The camp
theme sound great 'Soaking in Jesus.' It will do you good."

Reggie picked up a bag and yelled. "Charles, I mean
Chuck. You ready?" She didn't really care about him driving with them but she was glad he was there to carry her
luggage.

***

Mindy hugged Elizabeth as soon as she walked in the
door. "I'm so glad to see you. Was it awful?

Elizabeth nodded.

"Come on in the kitchen and we'll have tea and you
can tell me about it before we start working."

Elizabeth described her discovery of Hanley Drew's
body and also the interviews with the police. Then she sat
up straight. "I just thought of something."

"What?"

"Hanley didn't have any make up on. That shows she
wasn't killed right there as soon as she left the stage. All
that green witch make up takes a long time to get off!"

Mindy's eyes narrowed. "I'm trying to remember. Charles and I came on opening night so it's been a couple of days but there wasn't a lot of time after the witch melted 'til the play was over, was there?"

"No, but I'm not sure how long. I told the police about fifteen minutes. But I could be wrong. Ron Lockland will figure it out. He's the stage manager. Poor thing. He's been in love with Hanley forever. He was too upset to even think at the time."

"Are you going to call the police? To tell them about the makeup?"

Elizabeth thought of the Deputy's bet and forced herself not to smile. "No, not yet."

Mindy was looking thoughtful. "Who would be eliminated?"

"Dorothy. That's a great help, isn't it? I can't see Margaret Brock in the role of first murderer." Elizabeth gave Mindy a wry smile. "Really, she was the only one that was on stage all the time from the time the witch melted. They sang 'Ding Dong, the Witch is Dead,' went back to the Wizard, Dorothy misses going with him in the balloon, and then she does the heel clicking thing and ends up back in Kansas and it's just a few minutes 'til it's all over." She grinned. "Hey, Glinda the Good could have done it right after the melting and before she came on. No, the makeup would have taken longer. So Reggie is cleared too!"

"But she wasn't in the last scene, was she? I mean I don't suspect Reggie for a minute. But wouldn't it have to be somebody not in the last scene?"

Elizabeth nodded. "Leaving out the Munchkins and other kids, that would leave the stage crew, the Wizard, the Tin Man, Cowardly Lion, and the Scarecrow."

"And they would be?"

"Albert Shaw was the Wizard, he's the friend that came down with Cal Morgan from New York."

"Would he have had a motive?"

Elizabeth shook her head. "I can't think what...well, unless Linda is right and he's in love with Cal Morgan and was jealous of Hanley. No, that's not right. They admitted to the police that she got Cal to pretend that they had a relationship. I guess to keep Ron from getting his hopes up."

"And the others?" Mindy prodded.

"The Tin Man was played by David Sutton, the youth pastor from First Baptist Church. I honestly don't believe for a second he had anything to do with it. The Scarecrow was Lisa Coulter, Hanley's best friend; they grew up together. She's the one that got Hanley to come for the show."

"There you are!" Mindy clapped her hands. "She got her here and killed her because...because she was jealous of Hanley being famous when she was stuck here in Simpsonton being an amateur."

Elizabeth wasn't convinced. "And the Cowardly Lion was a guy named Bob Crawford who came because his little girl tried out and was cast as a Munchkin."

"He was really good. I remember he made me laugh."

Elizabeth nodded. "We don't know that he had or didn't have a personal relationship of any kind with Hanley Drew. But I guess we'd better start asking around."

"I thought the FBI and State Police were handling that." Mindy grinned at her.

Elizabeth grinned back. "Well, it won't hurt."

Then Mindy brought in the letters and they agreed on some more responses.

***

The car was parked where the driver could clearly see the kids leaving the movie theatre, even though the rain made a curtain of water and blurred the picture. The umbrella Sara Conley's companion held over them both was masking her face but surely it was the Tate girl. Not many people there on a Monday night. What a smart idea to watch the Conley girl's home and then follow her.

The driver watched while the other few patrons went their separate ways and only the two girls were left waiting on the corner. After looking both ways to insure no one would see the car, the driver started it.

Swerving up on the curb, the car hit both teens head on, backed off, and sped away into the night.

***

Reggie tried and tried to get comfortable on the cot. But nothing seemed to work. She didn't want to be here. And that made her sad. She looked forward to this camp experience for months and now it seemed a waste of time. She wanted to be back home.

No, she admitted it to herself. She wanted her mom. And as soon as she admitted it, the tears sprang to her eyes and would not be repressed.

Reggie bit the pillow and held back the sobs that threatened to spill out into the near-silence of the cabin. Camp was just too soon after the shock of Hanley Drew's death. Her murder.

When they decided that she would change dates it seemed like a good decision. She wouldn't be able to come with the rest of the youth group on the church bus Sunday afternoon and she would miss the first night but that didn't seem like a big deal. Not then. But this afternoon when her Mom brought her here, just a ninety minute drive from home, she felt like an alien or something. The other kids seemed so...so young. They hadn't been working with New York actors. And they hadn't been involved in a murder.

Reggie thought back over the last performance. Did anything happen that would be a clue to who killed Hanley Drew? Anything that she and Sara hadn't thought about?

She couldn't think of anything different from every other performance. She let each scene play out in her mind from the beginning. *That's silly. It doesn't matter 'til the end. That's when it's important.* The Wicked Witch of the West had melted away before the final two scenes. And she went straight to her dressing room as far as Reggie knew. *I wonder how long she was in there dead before Ms. Daily, Mrs. Delaney, found her?*

Reggie hadn't seen the body but just the idea of it sent cold chills over her body and made her stomach turn. Suddenly she wished someone else was awake. Preferably the Cabin Counselor. But she could hear gentle snoring coming from the lady's cot right by the door and knew she was alone in her wakefulness.

Reggie was off stage until after Dorothy met the Wizard. She sat in the wings, across the stage from her mom and Mrs. Delaney and Ron Lockland, awaiting her cue. *Was anything different?*

Everything on stage was the same. The wicked witch was melted. And then Dorothy, Toto, Tin Man, Scarecrow, and Cowardly Lion went back to see the Wizard. What was going on back stage? She went over every detail in her mind. The younger children were in the band room awaiting curtain call, being watched over by some of the parent volunteers. The stage crew, Mr. Lockland and some of the parents, changed the scenery, transforming the witch's castle to outside of the Wizard's hall. Margaret came over to stand by Reggie during the scene change. She couldn't remember seeing Mr. Sutton or Mr. Crawford or Ms. Coulter. Mr. Morgan was moving around whispering to the tech crew on his radio system. Mr. Shaw followed him some of the time, but then came and stood by Reggie to watch. When it was close to time for his cue, he went back stage and crossed over in order to make his entrance from the other side of the stage. *How long did he take to get from one side to the other?* She couldn't remember. It wasn't important to notice at the time. And Mr. Morgan was wandering around a lot.

The person responsible for Ms. Drew's death must be one of the men from New York. It just couldn't be somebody from home. *Could it?*

The last time Reggie checked her watch, it was 2:45. And reveille came at 6:30 a.m.

***

Linda Tate opened the paper that Chuck brought to her that Tuesday afternoon. The death of Hanley Drew was still front page news although it didn't take up as much space as the Monday edition. Then she gasped.

"What's wrong, Mom?" Chuck turned back from the refrigerator.

"Sara! She was hurt in a hit and run accident last night near the movie theatre. Another girl with her, a Judy Sinkhorn, was killed."

Chuck looked shocked. "Why would anybody want to do that?"

"I don't know. But I'm so glad that Reggie is off safe at camp. Sara actually called her and asked her to go to the movie with them." She turned to pick up the phone book. "I'm going to call the hospital and see if someone can tell me how she is. This says she was in serious condition. I think that's better than critical but still..." Linda's voice trailed off. She realized she was rattling. *What if it had been Reggie?*

***

Elizabeth's cell phone rang and she smiled when she saw it was Linda Tate's number. She was enjoying having a good friend near her own age.

"Hey! What's going on?"

"Oh, Elizabeth."

The smile quickly faded as she recognized the distress in her friend's voice. "What's wrong?"

"Have you read the paper?"

"No." Elizabeth never read newspapers.

"Sara Conley was injured by a hit and run driver last night and is in serious condition."

"Oh, no! They have any idea who could have done it?"

"Evidently not. But, Elizabeth, there was another girl with her. And that girl was killed."

"Oh, Linda. How awful!"

"I feel guilty for being so glad that Reggie is off at camp. If she wasn't she would have gone with them to the movies. That's when it happened, as they were leaving."

"Don't feel guilty. You'd be an unnatural mother if you weren't glad your child is safe!"

"Elizabeth, you don't think...? Would you mind if I came over for a few minutes?"

"Not at all. Galen's gone back to work today."

"I'll be right there."

When Linda arrived, Elizabeth hugged her and led her into the kitchen where a pot of chamomile tea was steeping. She could see that Linda's hands were shaking as she put sugar in her teacup.

"Bless your heart. What a terrible shock."

Linda nodded. "Yes, horrible, but the worst of it is that I'm afraid it's tied in with Hanley Drew's death."

"What? Why do you think that?"

"I don't know. I just was worried that maybe Sara saw something that afternoon and was run down to shut her up."

"But if she had seen anything, she would have told the police."

"Not if she didn't realize it was important. You know. Oh, maybe I've watched too many TV shows but..." Linda took another sip of tea. "Elizabeth what I'm really scared about is what if Reggie saw something and the killer thought she was with Sara."

"Oh, Linda. Surely not. I think you are just..." Elizabeth stopped herself. *This is her child she is afraid for. Don't belittle that fear.* "I don't want to believe that. I hope it's not true."

"Me too. But...oh Elizabeth. I want to drive up to the camp right now and get my child and keep her safe. But then I think maybe she's safer there."

Just then Elizabeth's cell phone rang again.

It was George Tate. "Is Linda there?"

"Yes, here she is." Elizabeth handed the phone to her friend.

She saw Linda nod and take a deep breath. "Okay. I'll be right home."

Linda pushed the off button and looked at Elizabeth. "I think I'm relieved. George said Reggie called from camp and wants to come home. We're going to leave now."

"Good. I know you'll feel better when you have her with you. And she'll be safe here."

Elizabeth watched Linda hurry through the gate leading to the rest of the Court and her heart ached for her friend. How very vulnerable it must be to be a mother. Then her heart ached for a different reason.

Chapter Seven

"It seems like this drive is taking years!" Linda finally broke the silence. "I don't mean I want you to speed. It's just in my head that it seems like forever." She knew George didn't quite understand her fears but he was going as fast as the law allowed. And she really wouldn't want him to go faster on the curvy mountain roads.

"It's been a rough week." George reached over and squeezed her hand before putting it back on the steering wheel.

Tears came to Linda's eyes at the kindness in his voice and his gentle gesture. *I can't cry again! I've got to be calm when we get there.*

"I'm so grateful that you're in town this week!"

"Me too." George's voice sounded grim. Maybe he understood more than she had credited him with.

The sun was almost down and totally obscured by the tall pine trees when they turned into the last little one lane road leading to the camp.

"So, have you decided what we should do about Sara? Do we tell Reggie or not?"

George's mouth tightened. "I don't see how we can keep it from her, Sweetheart. She's going to hear it sometime and for us to not tell her would be..."

"Yes, you're right. She'd be very upset. But we don't have to tell her tonight, do we?"

"No. Let her come home and get a good night's sleep. I've decided to go in late tomorrow and we'll talk to her together."

Linda's heart leaped and she put her hand on her husband's shoulder. "Oh, thank you! I'm so glad I don't have to do it alone."

They parked the car and walked up the hill to the lodge where the Camp Director said Reggie would be waiting for them. As they climbed the wooden stairs, before they even reached the porch, the door burst open and Reggie came running toward them.

"Mom! Dad! I'm so glad...!" Reggie managed to hug them both at the same time, almost knocking Linda off balance.

They didn't say anything but Linda was sure the three way embrace told their daughter that they felt the same gladness.

When they broke apart, Linda saw the Director standing in the doorway observing them. George went over and shook his hand.

"Thank you so much for calling us. Reggie isn't usually a quitter but..."

Steve Johnson held up his hand. "No need to explain. That must have been a real ordeal, having a murder of someone you'd been working with closely. I'd probably react the same way."

Reggie turned back to him. "Will you let me come back next year?"

"Of course, Reggie. We'll look forward to it." He hugged her.

George carried the suitcase and duffle bag to the car while Linda and Reggie followed, arms entwined.

"Oh, Mom. I missed you so much last night! I just couldn't go through another night like that."

"Hey, I missed you too. I was relieved when they called and said you wanted to come home."

"I was afraid you'd be mad."

"Just the opposite, sweetie." She leaned over to kiss her daughter on the cheek.

When the luggage was stored in the trunk, they began the trip back to Tapestry Court.

***

Disgusting! The newspaper lay where it was thrown. *The wrong girl killed. The gods be thanked there were no witnesses. Unless the Conley girl saw the car before it hit her. And recovers. And remembers.*

Was there any way to insure that she didn't recover?

There were several possibilities. But which one stood the best chance of working?

***

Sara Conley woke up in the strange bed with the awareness that there were needles in her arms and a terrible pain in her left side. *What happened?* She looked around the darkened room and realized she was in the hospital. But why? There was an empty bed beside her and no one was in the room.

"Somebody?" She called but could tell that her voice was so weak that probably no one heard her. This was scary. *Wait, they always have a button to call nurses on TV.* She lifted her head to look for the button and waves of nausea caused her to let it fall back on the pillow. But in the brief moment of expanded vision she had seen a tube tied to the bedrail with a button attached. She reached out with her left hand, grabbed the button, and pushed.

In under a minute, a nurse appeared in the doorway. She came quickly to the bedside. "How are you feeling?"

Sara looked at the sympathy in her eyes and burst into tears. Then she wished she hadn't because it made her head hurt horribly.

"Why?" She asked the question through sobs.

The nurse took Sara's hand in her own and stroked it. "You were in an accident, honey. Do you remember?"

"N...no." Sara knew better than to shake her head.

"You were coming out of the movies and got hit by a car. You had to have some surgery but you are going to be fine. The doctor said you did really well."

"Mother know?"

"Yes, she was here earlier but had to go to work."

"When?"

"When did she...oh when was the accident? It was last night. You were brought in by ambulance around 10 last night and they did surgery early this morning. It's midnight now. I'm really glad you're awake." The nurse smiled. "We were beginning to call you Sleeping Beauty."

"Can't remember."

"That's okay. Don't even try. It's normal with that kind of trauma."

"What surgery?" The fewer words used, the less the head hurt.

"You had a ruptured spleen and they removed it. It's okay. Lots of people have their spleen removed and never notice. A good friend of mine had the same thing happen when she was seven years old. She's now forty-seven and never had any after effects at all."

Sara breathed a sigh of relief. Then she realized that she had been squeezing the nurse's hand very tightly. She loosened her grip. "Sorry."

The nurse patted her hand again. "It's okay. I'd be scared too. But you really are going to be fine."

"Remember?"

"Will you ever remember the accident? I don't know. Some do, some don't."

"Head hurts."

"Yes, there was a slight concussion but nothing serious. No swelling or anything."

Sara closed her eyes. "Home?"

"I don't know. It will be a few days. The doctor will be here around seven in the morning and he can give you a better idea."

Sara opened her eyes again. "Thanks."

"That's my job. If you need anything, you just push that button. Do you want some water?"

"Little."

"I'm going to roll up the bed slightly so you won't have to move your head." Sara could feel the bed moving her upwards from waist to head. That felt better.

"Better."

"Then we'll leave it up. Here you go."

The straw slid between Sara's lips and the cool water felt wonderful to her mouth and throat. When she had all she wanted, she held up her left hand and the nurse re-moved the paper cup.

"I'm going back to the station now. If you need any-thing, just push the button. Okay? And my name is Mar-gie."

"Okay!" Sara closed her eyes again and returned to the refuge of oblivion.

***

"Mom?" Reggie looked in horror from her dad to her mom.

"We're so sorry, Sweetheart. But the good news is that I called the hospital before you came downstairs and Sara is awake and doing well. She can have company and if you want, your dad and I will take you to see her this after-noon."

Reggie's stomach did a flip-flop. *What if she looks weird or something?* "Do you think she'd want me to come?"

She saw her parents exchange a look.

"Yes, I think it would be good." Her mom hesitated. "When I talked to her nurse, she was very pleased that someone had called about her. She said that Sara has been all alone most of the time and thinks it would be really good for her to have someone come and visit."

Tears sprang to Reggie's eyes. "Poor Sara." She nodded. "Yes, let's go."

Then she turned to her dad. "You're not going to work today?"

"Nope. I decided to take the day off and spend some time with my girls."

"Where's Char...Chuck?" Reggie was finding it hard to remember to call her brother the nickname he loved.

"He is with Ben Montgomery from school. He was invited to a sleepover last night for Ben's birthday and then a bunch of them are going swimming."

Reggie smiled for the first time that morning. "Hey, you mean I've got my parents all to myself today?"

They laughed. Her dad said, "I guess it's been a long time, huh?"

"Yeah, like maybe since I was four?"

"Tell you what. Let's make it a really special day. What about lunch at Lourey's?

Reggie's eyes widened. "Wow! That *is* special. I've never been there." Then she narrowed her eyes in mock accusation. "You went there when Great-Aunt Emily died but you wouldn't let us go!"

"You would have been bored."

***

They were seated at a table by a window overlooking the lake and studying the menu when Linda noticed the men sitting at a nearby table.

"Don't say anything but glance over at the third table to your right. It's the guys from New York, Hanley Drew's friends."

Reggie and George both followed her instructions. Reggie shuddered.

"I was thinking about it that night at camp when I couldn't sleep. It just has to be one of them. And I think it's the Wizard, Albert whoever. He had to go backstage to cross over to the other side for his cue. And he could have done it then. Nobody would have noticed how long it took him."

Linda looked over at her husband.

"I think we ought to leave the speculation to the police." George changed the subject. "So, have you decided if you're going to join the drama club at school this year?"

"I think so. I was going to for sure and then after Ms. Drew...well, then I wasn't sure if I want anything to do with theater. But I think so..."

Just then the two actors got up to leave and spotted them.

Cal Morgan walked over toward their table followed closely by Albert Shaw. He nodded solemnly. "How are you today?"

Linda nodded to the two men. "Fine, how are you? Have you met my husband?"

After introductions were made, Linda asked how long the men would be in Simpsonton.

Cal answered her with thinly veiled disgust. "The police said this morning that they think we can leave tomorrow. They've verified where we can be reached in the city and are no longer afraid we'll vanish. But we're going to stay for the funeral. After all we were friends with Hanley."

At least you were employees. But she said, "I know you'll be glad to get home."

"Yes, very glad. Who would have guessed that something like this would happen? Hanley was so vitally alive." Cal shook his head.

As the two men walked out of the restaurant, Albert put his hand on Cal's shoulder and patted him. For some reason the gesture surprised Linda. But it shouldn't have. She remembered her first impression that Albert was in love with Cal. She didn't think Cal was really upset by Hanley's death. But maybe the pat was for their benefit.

"So what do you think, Dad?" Reggie looked at her father eagerly. "Don't you think it was probably Mr. Shaw?"

George grimaced. "You aren't seriously asking me that question, are you?"

"No, I guess not. I mean, you couldn't really tell by just meeting him once."

Linda was sorry their special lunch was spoiled by the presence of the men which reminded them of the tragedy. She hadn't realized they were still in town. She really hadn't thought about them at all. The shock of Sara's condition had driven a lot out of her mind. And if she ever knew they were staying at Lourey's, she'd forgotten it.

The food was good, though, and Reggie seemed to enjoy herself and the company of her parents. She loved the built-in aquariums and when they went out to the dock at the back of the restaurant, she enjoyed the view of the lake. They stopped by the gift shop on their way out and George bought Reggie a bracelet she admired.

"Could we get something to take to Sara?"

"Certainly," George said. "Pick out something you think she would like."

"I think she'd like a bracelet just like mine."

"Then let's get it."

On the way back to Simpsonton, they did not mention Hanley Drew or her New York friends. It was a very pleasant drive, but when they turned in to the hospital parking lot, Reggie reached up between the seats and grabbed her mother's arm.

"Mom, you're going with me, aren't you?"

"Of course. We both are."

When they passed the flower stand in the lobby, George stopped.

"You're giving her the bracelet, Reg. What do you think, Linda? Want to pick out a flower arrangement from us?"

"Great idea." And she headed immediately for the glass front unit that had a little teacup filled with tiny roses and other flowers sitting there among the other arrangements.

"Isn't this different? Do you think she'd like it, Reggie?"

"Yeah, I guess. But I think she'd like this one better."
Reggie pointed to a bear wearing a University of Kentucky
shirt holding a bunch of daisies and a balloon.

"A UK bear it is!" Linda took the bear to the counter
and George paid for it and two get well cards which she
and Reggie filled out.

They took the elevator up to the third floor and found
room 318 with no problem.

When they walked into the room, Sara's eyes lit up.
And then filled with tears which spilled down her cheeks
before anybody said a word.

Linda's heart ached for the girl and she immediately
went over to the bed and hugged her as best she could
over tubes and needles.

"Oh, Sara, we're so sorry about your accident."

Reggie came up to the bed more shyly than her mother. Linda stepped back so her daughter could stand next
to her friend. Sara held out her hand and Reggie took it.
The tears kept flowing.

"I...I'm sorry. I'm just so glad to see you."

"I'm glad to see you too, but not here." Reggie smiled
sympathetically. "How long do you have to stay?"

Sara shook her head and started crying harder and
then grabbed her head. "Crying makes my head hurt."

George joined them at the bedside. "Then, young lady,
if it makes you hurt, I demand you stop crying right now!"

That made Sara laugh and the tears stopped. Linda
and Reggie laughed with her.

"I'm going out here for a few minutes. I'll be back." And
George left the room.

Linda wondered what George was doing, but soon
switched her attention back to Sara. *What kind of a mother would leave her child like this? Alone in a hospital!*

"Where is your mom, Sara? Did she have to go to
work?"

As soon as the words were out of her mouth and saw
the look on Sara's face, she wished she hadn't said them.

Sara shrugged. And then winced. "She's too busy. She's always too busy."

The tears started again and Linda immediately bent over and kissed the girl on the forehead. But she didn't say anything. *What is there to say?*

"So, when do you think you'll be able to go home?" Reggie sat down on the end of the bed and then jumped up? "Sorry! Did it hurt when I sat down?"

"No," Sara said. "And I don't know when I can go home. What's today?"

"It's Wednesday. The accident happened night before last." Linda answered her.

The door opened and George stuck his head in and motioned for Linda to join him in the hallway.

When the door closed behind her, George shook his head.

"Her mother has only been here once. The nurses say the child just lays there alone. They say she's healing well and will probably be released in a day or two. But they're concerned about what kind of care she'll receive when she leaves."

They looked at each other meaningfully.

"As you do to the least of these..." Linda left the scripture quotation unfinished.

George nodded. "I know. That's what I was thinking. I'll find out how to contact her mother and we'll go from there."

They looked at each other again and hugged before turning away.

Linda slipped back in the room just in time to hear her daughter.

"What happened? How did you get hit?"

"I don't know. The last thing I remember was sitting in the movie with Judy...Judy Sinkhorn. Remember, I called and asked you to go too. I was so excited about going to the movie that I forgot you were just leaving for camp."

Sara suddenly looked alert. "Hey, why aren't you at camp. And I wonder if Judy was hurt too? Do you know?"

Before Reggie could answer, Linda interrupted, acting as if she had just entered the room.

"I'm back. George is out there making sure you are going to get the best care possible!" She smiled at Sara.

But the girl was not to be deterred.

"What happened to Judy, the girl that was with me? Was she hurt too?"

Now what? I can't lie to her.

"Yes, Sara. She was. I'm sorry."

Sara's eyes widened again. "What do you mean?"

I hate this! Where is her own mother?"

"Judy was hurt very badly and died before the ambulance reached the hospital."

Sara stared at her for a few seconds and pulled the sheet over her face.

Linda looked over at Reggie who rolled her eyes upward and with an expression of relief, mouthed, "Thank you."

And then she explained to her covered up friend why she wasn't still at camp.

***

Elizabeth pulled out a fresh sheet of paper and uncapped a black gel pen. *I love gel pens. They make such satisfyingly bold marks!*

Where to begin her list? The questions just seemed to pop out without any coaxing when she was trying to solve the problem of the Tapestry heir. But now she didn't even know where to begin to prime the idea pump. After staring at the blank page for a few minutes she made her first mark.

1.

Okay, now what? What is question number one? Who killed Hanley Drew? I wish it was that simple.

But she knew the question most on her heart, so she started there.

1. Is the 'accident" to Sara and the other girl related to the Hanley Drew murder?
2. If so does Sara know something about the murder?
3. Is Linda right about the attack being aimed at Reggie too?
4. What were Hanley Drew's relationships to the men from New York?
5. What was her personal relationship to people in Simpsonton?
   a.   Ron Lockland
   b.   Lisa Coulter
   c.   Brandon Cress
   d.   Glenda Taylor
   e.   David Sutton
   f.   Bob Crawford
   g.   Parents of the children in the cast
6. Was it possible that someone other than the cast and crew could have been backstage?

This is better! I must have used the right prime-er!

7. What was Hanley Drew's financial situation? Who benefits from her death?

Elizabeth looked at her list and laid it down with a sigh. "Well, it's a start."

Galen startled her by answering. "What's a start?"

She could feel her cheeks getting hot. "Oh, just a list of questions."

"Elizabeth!"

That tone of voice was the one her husband used the time he found out she was going to try to discover who murdered Guy Tapestry. He wasn't her husband back then but the disapproval was the same.

"What?"

"You're not going to get involved in this."

Suddenly she grinned. "Oh, but I have to."

Galen frowned. "What do you mean, you have to?"

"There's five hundred dollars riding on this and half of it is mine...if I discover the killer before the state or federal investigators."

Her husband looked at her like she had gone out of her mind.

She took pity on him and shared Deputy Collins' phone call.

After he laughed with her, he shook his head. "I'm serious. I don't want you getting mixed up in this mess. It's dangerous. And ugly."

She sobered too. "Yes, I know. And I'm afraid that it might not be over." She told him about Linda's suspicion that Reggie might have been one of the intended victims of the hit-and-run.

The following discussion about Reggie Tate's safety successfully diverted Galen's attention from Elizabeth's list.

***

Margie King was reading over the charts before she made her first rounds of the night. The Conley girl was doing very well. But then she frowned at the doctor's note. *He can't dismiss her on Friday!*

Margie got angry when she felt like patients were being discharged too soon. Insurance companies! It shouldn't be about money but about patient care. And she greatly feared that Sara Conley wouldn't get good care at home. Then she saw another note written by the day nurse. The Tate family was going to contact the mother about after care. Margie breathed a sigh of relief. *Thank you, Lord, that somebody cares about that child.*

When she looked in on Sara she thought the girl was asleep but then her eyes opened and she smiled.

"Hi."

"Hi, yourself. I see you are doing better. How's your side feeling?"

"Sore but okay. The best is that my head doesn't hurt as much."

"Did you have a good day today?" Margie took Sara's vitals while they talked.

The smile got brighter.

"Yes, my friend Reggie and her parents came by." She gestured to a bear in a UK t-shirt holding a balloon.

"That's cool."

Then Sara help up her left arm. "And Reggie gave me this bracelet. She has one just like it."

"How nice. She must be a good friend."

Sara nodded. But a tear slid down her cheek.

"What's wrong, honey?"

"I wish..." The child was visibly having a difficult time swallowing and trying to not cry.

"It's okay, if you want to cry."

Sara shook her head. "Makes my head hurt." Then she gave a little laugh. "Mr. Tate said I am not allowed to cry since it hurts me."

Margie laughed with her.

Sara swallowed again and breathed in deeply. "I wish I had a dad like that."

"What's your dad like?"

"I don't know. I never met him. And Mom works all the time. Or is partying with friends. It made me... I guess it made me feel sorry for myself to see Reggie and her parents together."

Margie patted her hand. "Well, it's okay to feel sorry for yourself sometimes. As long as it doesn't become a habit!" She winked at Sara.

"You're a nice lady." Sara yawned. "I think maybe I can go to sleep now."

"Do you need anything for pain?"

"I don't think so. Not yet."

"Just ring if you do."

Sara nodded and closed her eyes.

On her way out, Margie looked again at the UK bear and smiled. She turned it so that it faced the bed more directly. Then she made her rounds of the other rooms.

It was several hours later that she checked Sara's room again. The girl was in a deep sleep and Margie was glad she didn't need any more pain medication.

When she turned to go, she noticed that the bear was not in the position where she had left it. And laying next to the bear was a box of candy. *Candy delivery between midnight and 3 a.m.?* A warning bell went off somewhere inside. She picked up the box and took it out to the nurse's station.

A card attached simply stated "From a Friend."

After staring at the box for a long time Margie King slipped it into her bag.

Chapter Eight

Elizabeth kissed Galen goodbye when he left for work that Thursday morning, and then tried hard to interest herself in housework. She made the bed and halfheartedly dusted the parlor. Finally she did what she really wanted to do and got out her list. *I can't just sit and do nothing. Inquiring minds want to know...but where to start?*

The easiest place to start would be with Glenda Taylor. Visiting the library was a normal action, and wouldn't need an explanation. It was awkward to ask questions without credentials. During the search for the Tapestry heir, George Tate had given her permission but here there was no assignment from anyone except her own determination to investigate. She smiled as she always did when she remembered the phone call from Deputy Collins. *But I don't think that constitutes official approval.*

The temperature was in the nineties and with the humidity the heat factor was over 105. As soon as Elizabeth stepped outside she would have guessed it even if she hadn't seen it on the weather report before Galen left. It was the kind of day that she wished she had an air conditioned suit to walk from her air conditioned house to her air conditioned car, especially since she had to walk all the way to the Archer's store. And it seemed that lately heat was bothering her more. *Surely not hot flashes beginning.*

The panic at getting too old to have a baby grabbed at her stomach again with an intensity that surprised her.

Elizabeth entered the library quietly. Glenda Taylor was staring at the computer and didn't notice her presence until she cleared her throat.

Glenda jumped at the noise and then, seeing Elizabeth, sighed. "I'm sorry. I am really on edge these days."

"No wonder," Elizabeth said soothingly. "I think we're all nervy."

"Did you hear about the Conley girl getting hit by a car?"

"Yes, awful. I'm going by the hospital this afternoon."

Glenda smiled. "That's nice of you. I don't think she has much family support. Do you know that her mother didn't even come to the play?"

"I didn't. But no support - that's what I understand from the Tates."

"They seem like really nice people."

"Yes, they are." Elizabeth didn't tell her George and Linda were going to take Sara to their home when she was released. She didn't suspect Glenda Taylor of anything, but just in case the accident had been a murder attempt, it was better to keep Sara's whereabouts private. "Are you going to Hanley Drew's funeral tomorrow?"

"Yes. I'm going to close the library for a couple of hours. I thought that was the least we could do since she was here helping the community."

Elizabeth blurted out the question most on her mind. "Do you have any idea who could have hated her enough to murder her?"

She was surprised when a flush leaped to the librarian's face and spread to her neck.

"No. Why would anyone hate her? She was very nice to everybody. There has to be some motive we don't know about."

Why are you so flustered? But since she could think of no other acceptable questions to ask, she began browsing in the fiction section.

Elizabeth chose a volume containing three novels by Agatha Christie writing under the name of Mary Westmacott. She'd never read the other novels by that author, only the mysteries. As she checked out, she and Glenda agreed they would see each other at the funeral on Friday.

Elizabeth drove straight to the hospital. She stopped by the gift shop and chose a little teacup full of miniature roses and other tiny flowers to take to Sara.

When she peered in the room, Sara was awake and moaning. She went straight to the bedside.

"Sara, are you okay?"

"No. The pain...it's awful."

"Have you rung for the nurse?"

"Yes, but no one came."

"I'll be right back." Elizabeth went out to the nurse's station which was near Sara's room. A woman sat staring at a computer. "Excuse me."

The woman looked up and smiled. "How can I help you?"

"Sara Conley is moaning with pain. And no one has answered her call." Elizabeth pointed to the light outside Sara's door.

The woman's face turned pale. "I am so sorry. I was away from the desk for a few minutes and didn't notice." She turned and picked up Sara's chart from the pile laying there.

After flipping through the pages, she nodded her head. "Third day...that's usually the most painful. Actually the girl has never requested anything beyond the normal pain meds. But it's been ordered should she need it." She stood up and headed toward the medicine cabinet. "Tell her I'll be right there."

Elizabeth went back in the room. "The nurse will be right here with something for pain."

Sara's eyes were so full of misery that Elizabeth's heart did a flip-flop. She took the teen's hand. "I'm so sorry. It won't be long now." Just then the nurse came in with a syringe.

Within minutes, Sara's facial muscles had relaxed and she breathed a sigh of relief.

"That was awful. It hadn't been like that before, not so bad. I could handle it."

The nurse smiled at her. "You don't have to handle it. That's what pain medicine is for. In fact you should call for it at the first sign of it getting strong. Pain is easier to stop at the beginning, harder when it has gotten really bad."

Sara nodded. "Okay. I don't want that to happen again."

When the nurse left the room, Elizabeth moved back over to the bedside. "Is there anything I can do for you, Sara?" Then before the girl could respond, Elizabeth retrieved the teacup arrangement from the sink where she had placed it when she first entered the room. "I almost forgot. This is for you."

"How pretty. Oh, Mrs. Delaney, thank you." She took the teacup in her hands and turned it around gazing at each flower in the arrangement. "Everybody is so nice to me." Tears welled up in the large blue eyes.

"Sara, you're nice and that makes people want to be nice to you."

The tears spilled over and down her cheeks. "Thank you." Then she yawned.

"I think the medicine is going to help you go to sleep. Want me to go ahead and leave or wait 'til you fall asleep?"

"Wait, please."

Elizabeth waited. When the girl was sleeping soundly, she picked up her purse and left the room. She went straight to the nurse's station.

"Is Sara here alone all the time?"

The nurse nodded. "As far as I know. She had some company yesterday, a family. They were very nice and asked for her mother's contact information. I gave it to them because..." She paused.

"Because nobody else acts interested in the child?"

The nurse nodded. "Awful. And she seems like such a nice girl."

"Is it true you are going to release her tomorrow?"

The nurse sighed and shrugged her shoulders. "That's what the notation on her chart says. I think it's too soon myself."

Elizabeth left the hospital and drove home toward Tapestry Court. As soon as she was in the car, she called Linda from her cell phone. "I just left Sara. She was having a rough time, needed extra pain medicine. Make sure they give her a good prescription before you take her tomorrow."

"I intend to." Linda's voice conveyed a strong determination. "We'll go see her tonight when George gets home. And he will make sure that they have everything right for her release."

Galen's car was parked at the grocery lot when Elizabeth pulled in. She looked at the clock on the dashboard and frowned. It was two hours before his usual return.

She hurried to the house and called his name.

"Galen, where are you?"

His voice came from upstairs. "Up here. Not feeling well."

His face was flushed and he had the covers pulled over him when she entered the room.

"Sweetheart, what's wrong?" She threw the library book and her purse on the chair and sat on the edge of the bed.

He shook his head. "Don't know. Got sick after lunch. Finally came home."

Elizabeth put the back of her hand on his forehead. Then she walked to the bathroom for the thermometer.

"I don't want that." Galen turned away when she tried to put the glass rod in his mouth.

"Galen Delaney, don't make me have to treat you like a little boy."

That elicited a weak smile and he opened his mouth. In three minutes she read the thermometer.

"It's nearly 101 degrees. Have you had any aspirin?"

He shook his head.

Elizabeth went down to the kitchen and soon returned with a glass of ice water and two aspirin. "Here, take these."

When he had swallowed the pills and drunk half of the water, he fell back on the pillow. "Sorry to be trouble."

Elizabeth leaned down and put her head on his chest and her arms around his shoulders. "No trouble. I love you."

"Don't want you to catch it from me." He murmured in her ear.

"I won't. I promise." She lay there until she heard a quiet snore. Elizabeth withdrew from the embrace slowly so the change in pressure wouldn't awaken her husband and then she stood by the bed looking down. *Lord, heal him, please.*

She slipped out of the bedroom after placing his cell phone on the table where he could easily reach it. And she made sure she took her own with her when she went downstairs.

Even though the weather was hot, she decided to make some chicken soup. She'd heard it was good for people when they are sick. She put the chicken, originally intended for the barbeque grill, into a pot on the stove to boil. There would be enough for chicken salad as well as the soup, so whichever Galen was in the mood for, she'd have it.

She picked up the house phone in the library.

Linda answered on the first ring.

"It's me - Elizabeth. Galen came home sick this afternoon. He's got a fever of almost a hundred and one. I gave him some aspirin and water. And I'm making chicken soup. But what else should I do? I've never taken care of a sick person in my life. Well, not physically sick."

"What are his symptoms? Does he have pain anywhere?"

"I don't think so." Elizabeth tried to remember if Galen mentioned pain. "No, he just said he didn't feel well."

"If there's no pain, it may just be a virus. But if he starts to have pain anywhere, better call a doctor."

***

Margie King was frustrated. Her brother said it would be at least Monday before he could get the results of the test back from his friend at the lab. And that left four days where Sara Conley could be in danger and no one would realize it.

She picked up Sara's chart and flipped through 'til she found the name and phone number of the people who were trying to help the girl. *And what am I going to say? Hi, I stole your friend's candy because I was afraid it might be poisoned. I don't know if it was, but just in case... Just in case, what?*

They'd think she was an idiot as well as a thief. But she wrote down the information nevertheless. Then she turned back to the most recent sheet and saw that Sara was given an injection for severe pain twice that day. *And she's leaving the hospital tomorrow!* She determined to page the doctor before she went off duty to insure he understood the situation. Then she went to check on Sara.

The girl was sleeping peacefully, hugging a teddy bear to her chest. Margie patted the thin shoulder. *Lord, watch over her.*

***

Linda Tate pulled the couch bed out.

"Reggie, would you pull the sheets off for me? I can't remember who used this last or when. And lie down and see if you think the mattress is going to be comfortable enough for Sara."

Reggie stretched out on the bed and turned over a few times. "It feels fine to me." When she stood up again, she began detaching the corners of the sheet from the mattress. "What about pillows?"

"Oh, I'm glad you said that. They're in the front hall closet up on the shelf. Would you get them down and pull the cases off? I'll wash them with the sheets." Linda went to the laundry room and poured liquid detergent in to the machine. She waited until Reggie appeared at the door with the pillow cases and then added them to the sheets with a few towels she threw in.

The phone rang just as she closed the door to the washing machine and Reggie ran to get it. In a minute her voice rang out. "Mom, it's for you."

It was an unfamiliar voice on the other end of the line. "Mrs. Tate?"

When Linda assured her that she was, the woman continued.

"This is Margie King. I'm a night nurse at the hospital and I've been attending Sara Conley. I understand that you and your family are going to take Sara to your home for recuperation. Is that correct?"

"Yes. We're going to pick her up this afternoon. We have a funeral to go to in a few hours." When there was no response, Linda continued. "Is that still okay?"

"Mrs. Tate, I'm going to take a chance that you won't think I'm crazy. I wish we could talk in person but...I'm really worried about Sara."

Linda felt a clutching at her heart. "Is she worse? I know she was hurting a lot last night."

"No, she's no worse." The nurse's voice was soothing. "I hate it that she's being dismissed this soon but she's doing well and there will be sufficient pain medication prescribed so that she shouldn't be uncomfortable."

"Then what are you concerned about?" Linda hoped her voice didn't sound demanding.

"Okay, here goes. Night before last there was a box of candy in Sara's room. Did your family bring it by any chance?"

"No. We took a bear and a balloon and my daughter took a bracelet."

"Yes, I knew about those. Sara was very proud of them."

Linda waited.

"The thing is, the candy appeared somewhere between midnight and three a.m. It wasn't there earlier and then it was. And I got worried. You know. She was hurt by a hit and run and then that candy appeared in the middle of the night. Maybe I read too many murder mysteries but...well...I took the candy. I was afraid it might be poisoned." The nurse stopped talking and there was silence.

Linda didn't know what to say.

"Mrs. Tate? Are you still there?"

"Yes. I'm sorry. I was just shocked by the thought." Then she remembered how the lady opened the conversation. "And no, I don't think you're crazy. I've been worried too. That's one reason we asked to bring Sara here."

She heard a loud sigh come through the earpiece of the phone.

"Thank God. I gave the candy to my brother who has a friend who works in a lab. He'll know Monday if there is anything harmful in it."

"And you'll let me know?"

"Immediately."

"Can I take your name and phone number?"

"Certainly. And call me if you need me."

When Linda had written Margie King's name and number in her address book, the women hung up from their conversation.

"What was that all about?" Reggie was standing in the doorway.

Linda wondered how much she heard. She thought back over the conversation and realized that the parts that would scare Reggie were all on the other end.

"That was one of the nurses who's been taking care of Sara. It was so nice of her to call and offer to help any way she could."

When they finished the laundry and made up the couch bed, mother and daughter began getting dressed for the funeral.

"I haven't called Elizabeth." Linda picked up the phone again.

The phone at the Manor House rang six times before Elizabeth answered and she sounded out-of-breath.

Linda hastened to apologize. "I'm so sorry. I bet you were upstairs with Galen?"

"That's okay. He's so much better today. He's going to be fine. Must have been one of those twenty four hour viruses."

"I'm glad to hear it. Are you planning to go to the funeral?"

"Yes, are you?"

"Yep, want a ride?"

"You bet."

***

Elizabeth adjusted the scarf around her neck. It was a brown and black swirl design and looked appropriate for a funeral.

"You look pretty." Galen was propped up on pillows watching her get ready.

She smiled at him through the reflection in the mirror. "You're prejudiced."

"Sure am." He pushed the covers back with an impatient gesture. "I hate being sick."

"I hate you being sick too. But you are so much better. By tomorrow you'll be fine. Just rest today."

"I will. But I can't stay in bed."

She turned and narrowed her eyes. "If you go downstairs you promise you'll lie on the couch and watch TV or something? You won't work?"

"I promise."

When she kissed him goodbye, he was comfortably settled on the couch in the library propped up with pillows and engrossed in an old John Wayne movie.

When she looked at her watch, Elizabeth saw that she was a little early for the time she told the Tates she'd be there, so she opened the gate to the garden and sat on a bench near the central fountain with the giant T in the middle. The silence except for the bubbling water kept her from being able to continue pushing down the thought that her attendance at Hanley Drew's funeral had nothing to do with respect or duty. She was going for one reason only. To make contacts that would hopefully lead to interviews where she could find out more information.

Forgive me, Lord. Or is this your will that I am so determined to find out the truth?

She saw across the fence that Linda and Reggie came out of their house and looked toward Number One. She stood up and waved and then opened the gate to join them. The Tapestry Park garden had four gates. The one leading to the garage had been a locked one, inaccessible except to Court residents, until the renovation. The other three were regular gates leading to the Anderson's back yard, the Manor House lawn, and the Court proper.

"Pretty day." Linda Tate looked pretty herself, dressed in a coral suit that accented her red-gold hair. Reggie, dark-haired like her dad, was more subdued looking in a navy skirt and top.

Elizabeth agreed.

When they pulled into the funeral home parking lot, Elizabeth was surprised to see there were no spaces left. Linda pulled onto the street again and found a spot several blocks away.

"Lots of people are here." Reggie walked awkwardly in her heels on the sidewalk that sloped up to the mortuary.

Elizabeth guessed she was sorry there was not a closer parking place because of her shoes. "I'm surprised. I didn't think about her having that many friends here."

"It didn't seem like it during the time we spent with her, did it?" Linda paused on the walk and took a deep breath. "Hmm. I'm out of shape. It must be because she's famous."

"Could be. Or it could be that there are a lot of people here in Simpsonton who thought well of her when she was younger." Elizabeth waited for Linda to start walking again.

"Maybe." They turned into the parking lot and finally reached the door of the funeral home.

Every seat they could see that did not have a person in it was claimed by a purse or something else that showed it was taken. There was a small crowd milling around by the casket, but the Tapestry Court residents did not join them. After they signed the book, Reggie pointed to some men who were opening folding chairs and stationing them at the very back of the room. They hurried to get seated before those too were taken by the ever increasing crowd.

Linda whispered, "This has to be because she's famous."

Elizabeth nodded. "I think you're right." Elizabeth stood up to get a better view of the room. After all she was here to find out things.

Lisa Coulter was up by the body, greeting people. Elizabeth watched while she nodded and shook hands and hugged those who filed past. Ron Lockland stood with his back to them, hand on the casket, head bowed.

Seated on the front row to the right were the two men from New York. Elizabeth was surprised to see them. She assumed they would be back in the city by now. But then if Cal Morgan was in love with Hanley, of course he would want to stay for her funeral. But she remembered again what he said to the police. It was just pretense. Or was it? Maybe he was in love with her and she rejected him.

Someone sat down on the chair next to her and Elizabeth looked over to see David Sutton who played the Tin Man. He was alone; his fiancé didn't come with him. Reggie leaned up from behind her mother and waved at the youth minister. Elizabeth didn't see anything but friendly recognition in the gesture and was glad that Reggie was over her crush.

This was as good a place to start as any. She leaned over and said in a low voice, "I'd like to talk with you sometime when it's convenient." Sutton looked surprised but he nodded.

The mortuary attendants went and spoke softly to those who were up front near the casket and people began to sit down. Shortly the strains of 'Amazing Grace' filled the room furnished by some unseen organist.

The minister who officiated was obviously not acquainted with Hannah Drew and had not one personal thing to say concerning her. It was the driest funeral Elizabeth had ever attended.

Since they were at the back, they were the first to be directed up to file by the casket. Elizabeth normally avoided caskets but since it was the custom in the area she didn't want to appear rude by running in the opposite direction. When their small group reached the front, Cal Morgan caught her eye and nodded. She gave him a slight smile, trying not to be inappropriately friendly for the occasion.

After they filed out into the vestibule, most of the crowd headed for their cars which were lined up to go to the grave side service.

Elizabeth turned to Linda. "Are we going to the cemetery?"

"No. Unless you want to."

"No, not at all."

"I'm ready to go." Reggie plucked at her mother's sleeve. "Aren't we going to pick up Sara from the hospital?" She turned to Elizabeth. "She's coming to our house while she gets well."

"I know. That's very nice of you."

Just then Lisa, Ron, and the two men from New York walked by and Elizabeth nodded at them with what she hoped was a sympathetic look.

David Sutton moved into Elizabeth's line of vision. "Are you busy right now? I've got time to talk."

"Now's good. But..." She pointed to Linda and Reggie. "I rode with them."

"I can drive. We could go get a coke or something and then I'll take you back home...Tapestry Court, isn't it?"

Elizabeth thanked the Tates for the ride and followed David to his car, a white Suzuki. He opened the door for her.

"Thank you. This is a nice car. Bigger on the inside then it looks on the outside."

"Yes. My white horse."

"White horse?"

"Yes, I said a few years ago that next time I'm going to get a white horse so everyone will know I'm one of the good cowboys."

Elizabeth laughed.

Chapter Nine

When they were seated at Wendy's, Dave with a Frosty and Elizabeth with a Diet Coke, he opened the conversation.

"Now what did you want to talk about?"

"I want to know everything you know about Hanley Drew...Hannah. What kind of person was she? What were her faults?"

David scratched his head. "I don't..."

"David, I understand that you don't want to talk negatively about anyone. But we need to know everything we can about Hanley. The more we know about her life, the better we can understand her death."

He nodded, looking miserable. Elizabeth understood but she was relentless.

"You went all through school with her. What kind of thing could she have done that would make someone want to kill her – and in such a brutal way?"

"Call me Dave." He hesitated. "The only word that keeps coming to my mind is 'clueless.' "

"Clueless?"

"I mean, Hannah was just kind of clueless about other people. She was the 'Have' of all Have's and she didn't seem to notice that others around her were 'Have Nots.' "

His mouth twisted in a grimace. "That probably doesn't make sense to you but there was an incident in high school. A girl named Shelly was from a very poor family and she and Hannah were competing in the school pageant. I mean, there were lots of girls competing, but Shelly and Hannah were the prettiest and the most talented. Hannah did a monologue and Shelly sang - had a beautiful natural voice. They probably were tied in the talent department and natural good looks." The youth pastor shrugged. "But in the other aspects, Hannah had it all over her. Hannah's clothes were stylish, both her formal and informal outfits. And of course with those clothes and knowing she was..."

He gave a short laugh. "...'practically perfect in every way' like Mary Poppins, she was hands down the most poised. It was no shock really when Hannah won. Of course she didn't need the scholarship money, whereas the title and the money could have meant the world of difference to Shelly's future." Dave shook his head. "I'll never forget that night. I was the escort of one of the other girls and so I happened to be back stage after the pageant. Everybody was gathered around Hannah except for Shelly who was standing off to the side obviously choking back tears. Then Hannah said in a very loud voice, which carried over to where I was standing near Shelly, 'Well, I would have really had a difficult time winning if Shelly had even a little bit of taste in clothes.' "

Elizabeth's eyes widened.

He nodded. "Exactly. Clueless. I honestly think that was her way of trying to be humble. So I guess what I'm saying is that her inability to understand other people, or her callousness – that's it – callousness and insensitivity to others...could cause someone to hate her."

Elizabeth nodded. "So tell me about her friends."

Dave scratched his head. "Well, of course there's Lisa. We all, I'm embarrassed to say it, but we all made fun of Lisa. She trotted around after Hannah constantly. And to be fair, Hannah really seemed fond of her too. But we were all aware that Hannah was the strong personality in the friendship. Lisa was from a very average family, parents both worked until they died in an accident. Then she went to live with Hannah, but I'm sure you knew that. Lisa was quiet but very smart and she got a scholarship to college. I guess you know she became a teacher."

"What about Hanley's, Hannah's, family?"

"Only child. Parents both died within a year of one another sometime when she was in college. That's when she quit school and went off to New York. We all figured she got the inheritance and so could do as she pleased."

"Her parents had money?"

"Oh yeah! Lots and lots of money!"

Elizabeth was thoughtful for a moment. "I wonder what happens to it now?"

Dave shrugged. "She must have a will. The attorney or whoever would have insisted that she make one at the time she inherited."

"Yes, I'm sure you're right." She turned the conversation back to her first question. "And did she have other friends?"

"Not girls, not that I can remember. Girls never really liked her. Now, there were lots of boys after her." He gave a little laugh. "I wasn't one of them. I had a girlfriend from eighth grade on through high school and college - and just wasn't interested in other girls." He grinned. "You met her. She's now my fiance! But as far as friends, I guess Ron would be a friend. Although he was always nuts about her. Even though she never dated him, he never stopped hanging around her. So maybe I'm being unfair. Maybe they were just friends."

Elizabeth remembered the look of adoration she had seen on Ron Lockland's face as he looked at Hanley Drew that first night. And she doubted that there was just friendship, at least on his part.

"You probably wonder why I am being so bold asking questions but I'm a psychologist on sabbatical and I guess I'm missing the daily contact of human personalities and trying to figure them out."

Dave laughed. "Anytime you want, come to my youth groups, any of them - especially the high school one. That should give you plenty of material to puzzle over. And you could give me a few hints!"

Elizabeth smiled at him as they walked back to his 'white horse.' "I suspect you already have a few insights."

He opened the passenger door for her. "What do you mean?"

"You chose an interesting time to announce your engagement. I could see maybe at the cast party but..."

The young pastor's face flushed. "Yes, well, that was the original plan. But it seemed wise to do it then."

So he had noticed Reggie's crush! How kind as well as wise. She nodded. "Yes, very wise. Thank you."

He nodded.

He dropped her at the front gate of Tapestry Court and was driving off when she realized she didn't have her keys with her. She pulled her cell phone out and called Linda's number but there was no answer. Oh, yes, they would be going to pick up Sara from the hospital. She didn't have any of the other Court resident's numbers programmed in so there was no choice but to call Galen.

He didn't answer his cell phone either and she remembered he probably left it upstairs. When she called the house phone, he picked it up immediately.

"Hey Bits. Where are you?"

She laughed. "I'm stuck outside the front gate – forgot my keys."

"Where's Linda?"

"I got a ride from Dave Sutton, the youth minister who played the Tin Man. Linda and Reggie were going on to the hospital to pick up Sara Conley."

"Okay, I'll run upstairs and get some clothes on."

"I hate this, after making you promise not to do anything but rest today."

Galen laughed. "I don't hate it at all. This must have just been a twenty-four hour bug because I feel fine. Be right there."

The August sun was hot and it took longer for Galen to get there than she thought it would. Elizabeth was glad when she saw her husband coming down the walk.

***

The moonlight was too bright but there was no one stirring in Tapestry Court to be able to see the progress. There were no lights on in any of the houses. That was good. It was going to be tricky but it was necessary. And the gods were in control. Slipping from bush to bush, edging toward Number Four was easy.

Were both girls in the same room or separated? It would be tougher if they were together.

Peering through a front window, the intruder could see the sleeping form of Sara Conley on a pull out couch. The moonlight was being friendly, thank the gods. No sign of the other one. Good.

Just as the tools were pulled out and ready to dismantle the lock, a light went on. At the bottom of the steps, the Tate woman paused and peered into the living room. The Conley child moved and looked toward her. The voices were muffled but could be heard.

"Did I wake you? I'm sorry. I just wanted to check on you and see how you are feeling."

"I hurt. I've been lying here awake but didn't want to bother anybody."

"Sara, that's why I put the bell there on the table next to you. You should have rung it. I'll get the pain medicine now." Linda Tate disappeared.

The gods had not failed. The girl was awake and had a bell. It could have been disastrous. The intruder started the slow progress away from Number Four and back toward the garage.

It was a shame. It would have been better to get it over with now, before the girls had time to talk and compare notes.

***

Chuck looked out his bedroom window. It was late but he couldn't get to sleep. He'd heard his mom go down the steps and figured she was checking on Sara. He felt sorry for Sara, living in that place, and her own mother not even caring. And he didn't mind her staying with them. But for some reason it made him a little bit afraid.

Nobody said anything to him about Sara's wreck. But he got on line and read the newspaper accounts. It looked suspicious to him. A hit and run. Yeah, anybody would want to run after killing one kid and hurting another. But Chuck thought it was on purpose. And nobody had said anything about Reggie, but he wondered if whoever did it thought the other girl was his sister. It was raining and the driver wouldn't have seen very clearly.

Chuck might not get along with his sister, and yeah she was bossy. But the idea of anybody wanting to hurt her made him clench his fist. And he was determined to protect her.

He didn't really expect to see anyone when he looked out the window so he was surprised when he saw a figure pass by the fence to the park back to the Manor House and through that gate toward the garage site. For someone who didn't want to be seen, that was the smartest way. The light at the Court side gate of the park would show clearly anyone passing by. As it was, only a dark figure like a shadow could be seen. And it looked as though it was coming from the direction of the house that sat be-tween his and the Manor House, Number 2, where Miz' Emily used to live and now Hattie Griffin, her housekeeper, lived alone. Why would Hattie Griffin be having company this late? He glanced at his alarm clock. 2 a.m. No way.

The next morning, Chuck gobbled down his cereal and peanut and jelly toast and announced that he was going out.

"Where?" his mother asked. But he could tell she was distracted, with her mind more on Reggie's friend Sara than whatever he was going to do.

He shrugged. "Just around the Court somewhere. We've been so tied up with the play, I haven't seen anybody for a while. 'Cept there." He'd make it sound really good. "You know, Uncle Harold and Aunt Lucy, you know."

Mom just nodded as he'd known she would and he left from the back door. He'd just crossed behind Number #2 and turned toward the main walkway when a voice from a side window startled him. Scared him, if he was honest with himself.

"Hey, young Charles, what you doin' sneakin' around here?" He knew Hattie was just teasing him; she was kind of like a grandmother to him, having done most of the raising of his Dad and Uncle Charles.

"I wasn't sneaking, Miss Hattie. I was just..." What could he say he was doing? "I was just staying in the shade and out of the sun on my way over there." He pointed. "I want to see what all they've done on the garage."

The expression on the brown face looking at him from the window showed some doubt at his answer but she just smiled and waved him on.

He strode quickly to the walkway and turned back left into the Manor House Lawn. From there it was a few steps to the gate and into the park and through to the unfinished garage. He was sure from the angle of what he saw last night, this was the way the ... the what? Murderer? Thief? Inter-something? Interloper. Well, for sure a Trespasser. Nobody from Tapestry Court would have gone that way. This was the way the Trespasser went to get out. But what were they doing there? And who should he tell?

"Chuck! How are you doing?"

There was no sneaking around in Tapestry Court. That was for sure. He turned to see Mis Dailey, uh, Mrs. Delaney smiling at him. She had on gardening gloves so he guessed she was out working in the yard. Wouldn't you know it? But she asked 'how' not 'what' he was doing.

"I'm fine. Just going to look at how far they got on the garage. Wonder when they'll start working again?"

"I think this week. I'll be glad when it's finished." She wiped sweat off her forehead with her sleeve.

"Me too," Chuck said. Then he thought why not? "Mrs. Delaney, can I talk to you a minute?"

"Sure. Come on. Want a bottle of cold water? I'm ready for one."

"Yeah, that'd be great!"

Mrs. Delaney left her gloves on the back porch and they went through to her kitchen.

"Where's Mr. Delaney?"

"He's working upstairs. He's made himself an office in the spare room." Chuck remembered the spare room that was empty and figured it was that one, not the girly looking one.

"He's using a card table right now but wants to get a real desk in there. We know we'll be here another eight months."

"I hope you stay longer!" Chuck protested.

She smiled at him and got two bottles of water out of the refrigerator. "What about a doughnut?"

He shook his head. "I just ate breakfast." He took the cap off of his water and gulped down several swallows.

"Now, what did you want to talk about, Chuck?"

He frowned. "I haven't told anybody else this. But last night; it was about two o'clock in the morning and I couldn't sleep. I got up and looked out my window and saw somebody going toward the park. They didn't go through that gate but went into your yard. I figured they wanted to stay away from the light and were sneaking out of your gate into the park and to where the garage is still open."

Mrs. Delaney nodded and he went on. "I just went out of my house and behind Miz Hattie's and came over here and I'm sure that's the direction the ... the trespasser was coming from." He frowned and looked at her. "But why would anybody want to spy on Miz Hattie?"

"I don't know, Chuck. Who else are you going to tell about this?"

He shook his head. "I think just you. And you can tell whoever you want." He hoped she would understand. "I don't want to scare anybody."

"I agree. And I'll think really hard, and pray, about who to tell. And I'll let you know."

Chuck breathed a sigh. "Great." Then he finished off the water and stood up. "Thank you, Mrs. Delaney. Thanks a lot."

She stood up too and ruffled his hair. "You are very welcome. And please, come to visit me anytime!"

Chuck grinned. "Will do."

***

Elizabeth watched Chuck Tate run around the building and back toward the sidewalk. After a minute she went in the house and got the phone book.

The answer came quickly. "Loury's On The Lake. May I help you?"

"Could you connect me with the room of Cal Morgan?"

"I'm sorry, Ma'am. Mr. Morgan checked out yesterday. I think he flew back to New York later in the afternoon."

She hung up the phone. So much for the hope that the men from New York were the guilty ones. But maybe they didn't leave after all. She picked up the phone again.

"Sheriff's Department. Deputy Collins speaking."

Elizabeth explained who she was. "Since you've got money riding on my figuring this out, I wondered if you could find out something for me."

She could almost see the grin on his face. "Sure, Ma'am. What'cha wanna know?"

"I want to know if those men from New York have left yet. And if so when."

"Wal, Ma'am I happen to know the answer to that'en without asking around. They left from Lexington on the 7:15 flight last night. I drove 'em there myself. Chief of Police asked the Sheriff if we'd do it and he volunteered me. They give a pass to watch 'em get on the plane, and then I watched that plane take off."

"Thank you, Deputy Collins. I appreciate it."

"Anytime, Ms. Delaney. You onto the killer yet?"

"Not, yet, Deputy. Just eliminating suspects."

"Don't see how them leaving last night could eliminate 'em."

"No, you're right but it eliminates them from me being able to question them."

He laughed. "Yer right about that."

She hung up the phone, glad he was satisfied with her answer.

She wished she'd asked Chuck about the size of the person he saw last night. That was scary, to think about someone here in Tapestry Court, at night.

She hadn't wanted to say anything to Chuck but just because the person headed to her yard near the park fence from Number Two didn't mean at all that he's been spying on Hattie. He could have been anywhere on that side of the Court, Bill Sinclair's at Number Six, or Hattie's, or what she most feared. She thought the trespasser was probably checking out the situation at Number Four, the Tate's house.

Where Sara Conley was recuperating after being run down.

Chapter Ten

Galen was upstairs so she was safe to get into detective mode. Elizabeth sat with her list in front of her, and made notes when applicable.

1. Is the 'accident" to Sara and the other girl related to the Hanley Drew murder? *It looks like it, since someone was sneaking around Tapestry Court.*

2. If so does Sara know something about the murder? *If she does, I doubt if she realizes it. Or she would have told somebody.*

3. Is Linda right about the attack being aimed at Reggie too? *???*

4. What were Hanley Drew's relationships to the men from New York? *Employees, but why would she want to give the impression that she was in a romantic relationship with Cal Morgan?*

5. What was her personal relationship to people in Simpsonton?

   a. Ron Lockland - *friend, she was the object of his adoration.*

b. Lisa Coulter - *friend, best friend since childhood, like a sister.*

c. Brandon Cress - *anything personal? Ever? Find out.*

d. Glenda Taylor - *Why did she get flushed when asked what reason anyone would have to hate Hanley Drew?*

e. David Sutton - *Evidently nothing personal. I believe him.*

f. Bob Crawford - *Nothing evident. But could there be a past relationship he didn't want his wife to find out about?*

g. Parents of the children in the cast - *From what Margaret said, Hanley - Hannah Drew - was a cousin to her mother, Carolyn Simpson Brock. They didn't seem friendly - maybe some family problem?*

6. Was it possible that someone other than the cast and crew could have been backstage? *Where was Glenda Taylor? Ron Lockland took over once the show began. Where was the Director during the performances?*

7. What was Hanley Drew's financial situation? Who benefits from her death? *Surely the will would be disclosed shortly.*

Elizabeth let herself out the library door and headed toward the Fowler's home. *I didn't lock the door! But Galen's here. So?*

She went back, locked the library door from the inside, checked to make sure the kitchen door was locked, grabbed her keys from the rack, her cell phone, left a note on the kitchen table and locked the front door behind her - feeling great irritation all the while. One of the great advantages of Tapestry Court over living in the city was the feeling of security.

The situation with the garage had just been an inconvenience, until now. Now she felt that they were all vulnerable. Vulnerable to unknown intruders, unknown dangers.

She slowed down and turned into the Tate's walk. Linda opened the door with a welcoming smile.

"Come on in, Elizabeth. I'm so glad to see you. And the girls will be glad too."

Elizabeth could see a wide eyed Chuck behind her. He was shaking his head and she knew it was a desperate cry that she not tell his mother about what he saw. As soon as Linda turned to lead the way to the kitchen, she winked and shook her head.

Reggie and Sara were sitting at the table. Reggie was eating from a bowl of cornflakes and Sara was having what appeared to be cream of wheat.

"Hi, girls. How are you feeling, Sara?" The girl swallowed and then looked at Elizabeth. And smiled.

"So much better, Mrs. Delaney. Last night was awful but this morning I'm really, really better."

Linda went over to put her hands on Sara's shoulders. "She'd have been better last night if she'd called for pain medicine." She patted Sara's arm and then moved toward the stove? "Would you like a cup of herbal tea, Elizabeth?"

"No, thank you. I just stopped by on my way to the Fowler's, to find out if you've heard how much longer before the garage is finished."

Linda laughed. "Funny you should say that. George just called and said they phoned with great apologies and said they were pulling some men from another job and would start Monday morning and it should be completed by Wednesday."

Elizabeth felt her muscles relaxing and she hadn't even realized they were tensed. "That's great." Then she grinned. "But I guess we have to prepare for huge noise next week. It's a shame we can't go somewhere to escape." She realized she could go to her apartment in Lexington but there was no way she was going to desert Tapestry Court until it was safe for Sara and Reggie. "Oh, well. We'll survive." She surprised herself by going over to give Sara a hug. And then of course she had to hug Reggie too. She turned to Chuck but the look on his face declared that he was in big boy mode and didn't want any of that silliness. She mussed up his hair.

"You guys have a good day."

Linda walked her to the front door. She lowered her voice, obviously so the children couldn't hear her. "I know you probably think I'm over protective or something but I'm really worried about the girl's safety."

And it hit Elizabeth. She *could* go to Lexington, and take Linda and the kids with her. But her apartment was too small for all of them, especially with Chuck who would be restless stuck there with all the females.

"Linda," and she lowered her voice too, "Let me talk to Galen. I'm thinking maybe we could go to Lexington and stay at his house until they get the garages finished, then we won't be vulnerable here at home."

Linda breathed deeply. "Then you do understand."

Elizabeth nodded. "Yes."

***

Galen was surprised when Elizabeth knocked on the door facing. She never interrupted him when he was working.

"Can we talk a minute?"

"Sure, come on in." He stood up and got another chair, the straight chair, which he sat in so his wife could have the more comfortable desk chair. "What's up, Bits?"

She told him her concerns and her desire to take Linda and the children to his home in Lexington. Until she said it, he hadn't realized that somewhere at the back of his mind, underneath all the bank business, was that same safety concern for the children. He nodded.

"Let's see. You and I can stay in my old room. How will they split up for the other two bedrooms?"

Elizabeth breathed what was obviously a sigh of relief. "Probably the two girls in one and Linda and Chuck in another - unless Chuck wants to sleep on the sofa bed." She paused. "If that's all right with you?"

"Sure, if he doesn't mind me making noise in the mornings before I go to work."

Elizabeth got out of the chair and came over to hug him. "You are wonderful, Galen. I am the most blessed woman in the world."

He stood up and brushed her hair back where it had fallen over her forehead. "And I am the most blessed man." He chuckled. "I'll have..." He stopped to mentally calculate. "at least four days that I won't have to commute!"

Elizabeth frowned and pulled back to look at him. "Do you mind so much? Do you want to move back to Lexington now? Before the lease here is up?"

He hugged her closer. "No, my love. I really enjoy Tapestry Court and our life here. It's just since this murder business, I don't like to leave you."

She pulled away again. "I'm going to call Linda right now." She turned back when she reached the doorway. "Thank you so much!"

"Nothing to thank me for. It's just another adventure in the life of the Delaneys." And he watched as she made her way out into the hallway before he returned to his desk.

***

Linda answered on the first ring.

"Want to leave after church tomorrow? And come back Thursday? Since the garages are supposed to be finished Wednesday."

"Yes! Unless we can leave today and go to church up there tomorrow."

That would get them away from another night of possible danger. "I'd love that. Do you think you can get everything ready by then? And is Sara able to travel away from her doctor? I hadn't thought about that."

"Yes, she has enough pain medication for a week. Her Doctor's appointment is next Friday. And it won't take me any time to get clothes together."

"Then that's settled." Elizabeth looked at her watch. "It's two now. What time do you want to leave?"

"I'll talk to George but I'd like to leave after supper, if you're sure that's okay."

Galen didn't seem to mind the change of plans at all. He put the papers in his briefcase and snapped it shut. "Want to go out and eat?"

"I'd love it but I'd rather stay here with just the two of us for the rest of the afternoon. I've got chicken salad and some leftover chicken soup too, for supper."

He grinned, "Good thinking. We won't be alone for the next five days."

So they made the best of their time together.

***

They decided that Elizabeth would ride to Lexington with Galen while Linda and the children followed in her car. George walked with them to the Archer's parking lot.

"Why are we going, Mr. Delaney?" Chuck looked up at his neighbor.

"Adventures." Galen answered.

Elizabeth added. "Since we're all free for this week and school will start in two weeks, we thought it would be a great time to go to the Explorium - you know, also called the Lexington Children's Museum, and some other fun places in Lexington, maybe the Horse Park." She looked over at Sara, limping along between George and Linda who each had an arm around her and had an idea. "We'll rent a scooter for Sara so she won't have to walk but can go and have fun too."

Sara was exhausted by the time they got to Galen's Lexington house, a modern brick home in a nice subdivision near Hamburg Place shopping mall. She was ready to go to bed so Linda and Elizabeth settled her in.

When they got back to the living room, Reggie was looking uncomfortable. "Mom, I don't want to sleep with Sara. I'm afraid I'll hurt her while I'm asleep."

Linda turned to Elizabeth. "I hadn't thought about that."

"Maybe you could sleep with your mother?"

Reggie nodded her head enthusiastically and Linda looked at Chuck. "Do you mind sleeping on the couch?"

Galen smiled. "It pulls out to made a bed. I made sure I would have enough sleeping places for when my family comes to visit." He hesitated. "My old family. You all are now my new family." Elizabeth walked over to put her head on his shoulder.

Chuck looked gleeful. He picked up his back pack. "I can watch movies all night" he said as he pulled out a stack of his favorite dvds.

"Not tonight you can't," his mother corrected. "We go to church in the morning!"

"Oh shoot! I thought we were on vacation."

"Charles Tate! You don't take a vacation from God."

"But I thought we could from church."

Galen laughed. "There's tomorrow night, Buddy."

"Yeah." The boy still looked sullen.

Elizabeth gave Galen a worried look. "Do you have a bell of any kind?"

He shook his head. "No, why?"

"Since Sara is going to be sleeping alone, she'll need a way to let us know if she needs help, like to go to the bathroom. Or if she needs more pain medicine."

Linda's face turned pale. "You're right. I wasn't thinking and didn't bring the one from home. Tell you what. I saw a Walmart. I'll run out and get one now."

After she left, Reggie settled herself into a recliner with a book, Chuck got permission to watch one of his movies, and Galen turned to Elizabeth with a grin. "We may not be going to have a baby but here we are in our home with three children to care for." He hugged her.

She smiled at him but she didn't feel comforted.

***

"Ma'am, Ma'am, I'd like to check out these books." Glenda looked up with a start.

"I'm so sorry, my mind was wandering." She took the library card and the stack of books from the man standing there in front of the desk.

When he had gone, she returned to her musings. *When will law enforcement realize they didn't question me last week, a week ago today. She was glad they didn't at the time. She couldn't say she was sorry that Hanley was gone and her relief might have shown then. It was a shame she went that way but at least it was after the last performance.*

She hadn't seen Brandon since the funeral and that was only from across the room. Surely he didn't suspect her. Everyone knew that the director always sat in the audience during the performances.

***

Chuck loved the Explorium. It was one of the best places he'd ever been. Ms. Dailey joined him for some of the adventures but a lot of the time she sat reading her Kindle while he explored by himself. He was sorry Sara didn't feel well enough to go out of the house. She didn't go to church with them yesterday either so Mom had to stay home. He really was sorry she didn't feel like getting out and having fun but he was glad that Reggie decided to stay with her and Mom. He and Ms. Dailey... Mrs. Delaney ... they got along just fine!

After two hours, they took a break for lunch. Chuck had been wanting to talk about the murder.

"Thank you for not telling my mom about me seeing the guy sneaking around the Court the other night." He stopped with the fork half way to his mouth. "You didn't, did you?"

She grinned. "No sir. I promised and I didn't, but I sure was glad when your mom suggested getting away from Tapestry Court because the garages leave us exposed to the world."

He put the food in his mouth and when he had almost finished chewing, finished enough to be understood, he nodded. "I thought that was the real reason we came to Lexington."

"You are right, as usual. But we don't want the girls to suspect that."

"It wasn't an accident, was it? Sara getting hit by that car?"

"We don't think so, Chuck. I wish it was but..." Elizabeth's voice betrayed the sadness that she'd tried so hard not to show.

"But why? Do you think she saw something the night of the murder."

"I don't know, Chuck.

His eyes narrowed as he quickly swallowed the last bite of his hamburger. "Or do you think the murderer thought the other girl was Reggie?" He looked at her closely and could see that she did think so, but didn't want him to do the same.

She shrugged. "Who knows. I hope that's not true. But from what you saw, the murderer could have come to Tapestry Court looking for either of the girls."

"If he knew where Sara went after the hospital. Do you think they would tell anybody?"

She sighed. "No, I don't think the hospital would tell but they could have found out somewhere else."

Just then Mrs. Delaney's cell phone rang. When she finished digging it out of her purse, whoever it was had hung up.

"It's your mom," she said as she punched redial. "Probably wanting to know how late we'll be because of supper." And then, "Hello, I'm sorry. My phone was at the bottom of my purse as usual."

Chuck watched as all the color drained out of her face.

***

Elizabeth saw that her hands were shaking as she disconnected her cell phone.

"What's wrong?" Chuck asked.

Linda hadn't said not to tell him. And he already knew a lot, as well as obviously being able to see that she was upset.

"Well, Chuck. I don't know if I'm supposed to tell you or not. But before Sara left the hospital a box of candy appeared in her room somewhere after midnight, according to the nurse. She knew it hadn't been there earlier. There was no card or any way to tell who it was from. So the nurse took it, and gave it to someone that has to do with the State Police lab. And," she paused and sighed. "They just got the results back and the nurse called your mom. Every piece of candy had been injected with poison. Lethal doses of poison."

"Dang! Then it wasn't an accident - the car thing I mean."

"Looks like it wasn't."

Chuck tilted his head sideways. "Do you think my sister is in danger too?"

Elizabeth shook her head. "I honestly don't know, Chuck. I hope not."

After a short pause, she added, "But I sure am glad we're here instead of home at Tapestry Court. 'Til the garages get fixed and let us be safe again, I mean."

He nodded. "You don't think the killer could know where we are, do you?"

Elizabeth was startled. "I don't think so. I hope not. Surely none of those who know would tell." She thought over the list of people they'd told about their trip, even though they didn't tell the reason; there was Mindy and the Fowlers. She didn't think they would tell anyone, or have any reason to. Unless they were asked and it didn't seem like a threat to tell. And of course George knew but he knew why and wouldn't tell anyone. She picked up her cell phone.

"Linda," she said when her friend answered, "do you think we ought to tell Mindy and the Fowlers not to let anyone know where we are?"

She nodded. "Okay. You call the Fowlers and I'll call Mindy."

It was only an hour after lunch that Chuck announced he was ready to leave. He looked guilty when he told Elizabeth why. "It just doesn't seem the same, now that we know for sure - about the murder, I mean."

She hugged him. "I understand, Chuck. When this is all settled and everyone is safe again, we'll come back and finish all the adventures."

Chuck hugged her back but didn't say anything.

They stopped at a grocery on the way back and arrived at the house with lots of snacks, steak for five and everything needed to make homemade french fries.

Elizabeth announced "I figure we'll order in pizza tomorrow night..." and was interrupted by cheers before she could finish. "And if Sara feels like it, we will go out to dinner Wednesday night." More cheers followed. It was a relief that Sara's five day liquid diet was over and she could eat what she wanted - which turned out to be very little of even her favorite foods. But Chuck made sure nothing was wasted.

After supper, Galen and Elizabeth excused themselves and went into their own bedroom after Elizabeth gave a signal to Linda that she was going to fill him in on all the news. She didn't feel guilty for letting Linda and Reggie do the dishes since she had bought and cooked supper.

As soon as the bedroom door shut behind them Elizabeth threw herself into Galen's arms and buried her face in his shoulder. He hugged her for a minute and then gently pushed her back so he could see her face. "I take it this is not a 'let's make love' hug."

She smiled. "Unfortunately not." Then she told him about the poisoned candy and the calls to Mindy and the

Fowlers to make sure no one found out where the girls were staying.

Galen nodded. "Good thinking. I don't know of anyone else we've told. Wait...what about the Archers? Do they know?"

"No. If anyone knew about our cars being parked there, they'd see we are gone, but even if they asked, the Archers wouldn't know where to tell them."

"Then we just wait it out until Thursday."

"And pray that they really do finish the garage by then."

Galen nodded. And then grinned. "Anytime you're ready for a different kind of hug, just let me know."

Elizabeth grinned back. "I think after everyone else has gone to bed?"

He gave a huge false sigh and agreed. They were laughing and holding hands when they joined the others.

Chapter Eleven

It was five minutes before time to lock the library door, when it opened. Glenda Taylor's heart sank until she saw who came in. Then the words just bypassed her mind and came out her mouth.

"Brandon! How are you? It seems like it's been forever since I've seen you."

He nodded. "I know. We didn't really get to talk at the funeral." Then he grinned, "That was only five days ago. But I'm glad it seems like forever to you. It has for me too."

If hearts could really melt, Glenda's did. But she couldn't think of a response.

He broke the silence. "Want to go to supper?"

"I'd love it. Let me get my purse and sweater."

After the usual round of "Where do you want to go?"s and "I don't care"s and "You choose"s, Brandon turned the car around and said "How about Outback in Lexington? Or would you rather go to Red Lobster?"

Torn between Lobster Bisque and a Bloomin' Onion, Glenda hesitated. "You choose."

Brandon laughed and reached over to pat her shoulder. "Outback it is, then."

Glenda sighed a great sigh of satisfaction and relaxed to enjoy the evening she had feared to spend alone. They didn't talk on the way to Lexington but listened to the country music station Brandon had selected. When she first met Brandon, she would never have suspected him of country music - or the romance that always goes along with it. But he definitely was addicted to it.

They split their onion and each had the signature steak and salad and baked potato. It was after they finished the meal that Brandon opened the conversation about the murder.

"This is a really strange situation. I'm glad we both have alibis."

"How do you know I have an alibi? You have the Tate boy who was with you all the time."

"And you have the Queen of Stage Mothers."

She grinned, "And how did you know that?"

"Glenda Taylor, don't you know that I am aware of you and where you are every minute that I possibly can be. The front row can be seen from the light booth. And you never moved." He reached over and put his hand on hers. "You do know how I feel about you don't you?"

Tears filled her eyes. "Oh Brandon, I hoped but I wasn't sure. I ...."

"I love you, Glenda. Do you love me?"

"Oh yes. Yes, yes, yes!" She felt the tears slide down her cheek.

He moved his hand and wiped the tears away with his napkin. Then he laughed, "I hope I didn't get steak juice or onion grease on your face."

She laughed too. "Can I ask you why you waited - why I haven't heard from you for so long?"

"It didn't seem like a good time to make a declaration of love so soon after a nasty murder."

She nodded in agreement.

Brandon raised his hand to the waiter and when the check and tip were duly taken care of, he stood up and took her hand as they walked out.

"A warning, " he said in a serious voice.

"What?" She didn't think she had anything to be scared about but he sounded so serious.

"When we get to the car, I'm going to kiss you with one of those kisses that would go on a chart of the top ten kisses ever - if a kiss rate-er saw it."

Glenda laughed. "That definitely doesn't scare me off."

After the kiss, she assured him that he made the chart.

As they drove home, the conversation reverted to the murder.

"Since you were sitting by Carolyn Brock, you'd know - did she ever leave her seat? Especially during the last scene?"

"Are you kidding? And miss the last scene of Margaret's last performance? No, she never moved."

"Darn!" Brandon hit the wheel with his hand. "I would so love for her to be the murderer."

Glenda laughed. "I'm shocked. Why do you wish that?"

"Because her daughter is very talented and if she were in jail, we wouldn't have to put up with her during any more shows." He shook his head. "That woman is a real..." He stopped himself before he finished the sentence.

***

The call came from George Tate Wednesday evening giving them the go-ahead to come home. The garages were finished, the locks worked perfectly, and Tapestry Court was once again a safely gated community.

They all packed up their belongings and since Galen had to work on Thursday, Elizabeth decided to ride back with Linda and the kids.

It was great to be home, knowing they were all safe. Sara was able to walk upstairs and let them settle her into Reggie's room in the other twin bed. While the kids got themselves back in their house routine, Linda fixed some lemon herb tea for herself and Elizabeth.

"You know, it's awful. I left my cell phone number with Sara's mother but have never heard from her once. Do you think I ought to call her again?"

Elizabeth was quiet for more than a few seconds and then shook her head. "I'm trying to call on my psychological expertise about dealing with someone like her but either I never met or studied about anyone like her, or else it's just not surfacing. I honestly don't know."

Linda shook her head. "So sad. I guess I'll just leave things as they are for right now. We've got enough problems to figure out."

Elizabeth nodded as she sipped her tea. "Isn't that the truth? I have no clue who could have killed Hanley Drew. I hoped it was the men from New York but that doesn't seem very likely. Especially since the attacks on Sara."

"Do you know who has been cleared of all suspicion?"

Elizabeth smiled. "I know who hasn't. I'm one of them."

"What?" Linda looked horrified.

Elizabeth laughed. "Well I was the one who found her and could have done it when I went back to get her, according to the officer."

"That's ridiculous. Who else is still on the suspect list?"

"Not you, obviously, because you were with the kids. Let's see. There's the Lion, Scarecrow, and Tin Man - Bob Crawford, Lisa Coulter, and David Sutton. Then, I don't know about Glenda Taylor. Where was she during the play?"

"Hmm," Linda put a finger on her lips. "I don't know but it was plain for anyone to see she didn't like the way Hanley flirted with Brandon. That's a possibility."

"I hope not. I really, really like Glenda. But I'd had the same thought. And when I asked her who could hate Hanley enough to kill her, she blushed."

"And then there are the parents of the Munchkins. Anything there?"

Elizabeth shook her head. "Not that I know of." Then she sat up straighter. "But I thought of something the other day. Hanley's face had all the green makeup removed so she must have been in her dressing room some time before she was killed. That stuff's not easy to get off."

"And what about Carolyn Simpson Brock? Weren't they related? Could she have a motive of inheriting something?"

"I doubt it." Elizabeth shook her head. "They didn't seem to be interested in each other at all. I can't imagine Hanley leaving her anything. And that reminds me, what about the will? Was it read while we were away? I wonder if it's a big secret or something?"

***

Elizabeth got her car from Archer's and bought chicken tenders, potatoes, canned shelly beans, real cream, and butter. By the time Galen got home Thursday evening, his favorite meal was ready, except for putting the chicken tenders into the deep fryer.

He came in and kissed her, a nice long kiss. "It's good to be home."

Elizabeth could feel her face light up. "You mean even though we've been at your home most of the week?"'

"This is my home, Bits."

Her heart fluttered. "At least for a few more months."

He just said, "Hmmm." Then "By the way I have some interesting news. I got a call today from Hanley Drew's attorney. Her accounts are with my bank and it seems that Andrews, the lawyer, wanted me to help him set up a date, time, and place for a lot of people to get together to hear the will. She made a new one two days before she died."

"What? Why?"

"That I don't know but I do know he wants you and me, George and Linda, all the board of the theatre group, and the Brocks to be there."

"Wow! That's a shock. Interesting. Where do you think?"

"Well, I thought maybe we could ask Glenda Taylor about the library after hours. She's on the theatre board. What do you think?"

"I think that's a great idea. Are you going to call her now?"

"You're her friend. Why don't you call her?"

***

Elizabeth was amazed at how quickly the will reading was set up with everyone's agreement - Saturday afternoon at 5:30 at the library. She guessed it was the result of curiosity that came from the possibility of money.

The only child present was Margaret Brock. The Theatre Board consisted of Ron Lockland, Lisa Coulter, Brandon Cress and Glenda Taylor. The others gathered were the Tates, the Delaneys, and Tom, Carolyn and Margaret Brock.

Gilbert Andrews sat at the end of the two long library tables which had been put together as soon as George and Galen arrived.

"I know this is a surprise and I apologize for the delay. I was on vacation out of state and just found out this last Thursday when I returned to work about the unfortunate, uh, death of Hannah Drew. Hannah is, was, her legal name even though her stage name was Hanley. I have made a copy of the will for each person or family here. And will just go over the essentials with you now.

"Ms. Drew was very wealthy, due to an inheritance from her parents and also her great financial success as an actress. Her assets are both immediate accessible ones and investments. Together they are worth between fifty and sixty million dollars."

There were several audible murmurs in the room. Then the attorney continued.

As for the accessible money Mrs. Drew left a million dollars to her friend, Lisa Coulter..." A gasp came from Lisa at the pronouncement. "...a million dollars to Ron Lock-land, and eight million to Margaret Brock." At that last announcement, there were more gasps, especially from Carolyn Brock.

"The last money mentioned will be put in a trust which Ms. Drew designated should be overseen by Galen and Elizabeth Delaney until Margaret reaches the age of 21. For that they will..."

"That is ridiculous!" Carolyn Brock stood up. "Her parents should be her trustees!" Her husband put his hand on her forearm but she shook it off. "There is no excuse for this. I will get another lawyer."

Elizabeth noticed that familiar embarrassed look on Margaret's face. And felt the same compassion she always felt for the child.

Finally Carolyn Brock sat back down and the attorney continued.

Elizabeth noticed that Lisa Coulter was glaring. Was it at her or Carolyn Brock?

"For this responsibility on their part, the Delaneys will receive 1% annually of the trust total beginning on the day the trust is settled and on each anniversary thereof."

Elizabeth didn't look up but her shocked mind was calculating that their income from that alone would be eighty thousand dollars a year. No wonder Carolyn Brock was furious. But why all that to the child?

"In case some of you are wondering why the division of money should go as it does, Hannah Drew explained to me that Lisa Coulter and Ron Lockland had been her best friends when she was younger, and young Margaret is her fourth cousin. She watched Margaret closely during the rehearsals and performances and became very impressed with the child. She was also impressed with the loving concern Mrs. Delaney showed to the child, as well as knowing the professional banking ability of Mr. Delaney." He turned a page.

"Now for the investments and businesses. They have all been left to the theatre here in Simpsonton with the condition that it be renamed the Hannah Drew Theatre. And she specifically told me she wanted it to be Hannah, not Hanley, although that can be put on the posters underneath, if the board so desires. She wants the theatre to be able to begin paying their actors and actresses and to buy or build their own building. She designated Brandon Cress and Glenda Taylor as trustees and for this, they will each receive one twentieth of the profits of the investments and businesses left after what is cashed in or sold for use in the theatre annually." He placed the papers back in the folder and began handing the copies of the will around the table. "By the way, the two gentlemen from New York witnessed the will and Ms. Drew gave them each a check for five hundred thousand dollars in my presence. She said they also were good friends to her." After his briefcase was closed, he asked "Are there any questions?"

Nobody spoke a word but arose and filed out silently.

"Well!" Elizabeth looked at Galen as he opened the car door for her. "That was a shock. I guess it was a shock to everybody. Even Lisa Coulter let out a gasp when she learned she was left a million dollars. And," she couldn't keep from grinning, "it was obvious that Carolyn Brock was not only shocked but horrified at you and me being appointed executors over Margaret's trust. I wonder why she did that?"

"Because it's obvious to anybody that her mother doesn't care about Margaret; she would take advantage of her financially like she does in every other way - to forward herself."

Elizabeth shook her head. "Sad. And Margaret is such a sweet child. It's really strange that I was never around children much and didn't particularly care but first there was Chuck and then Reggie, and Sara and Margaret." Then she realized that a strained look was coming over Galen's face so she changed the subject. And smiled. "So what are we going to do with the rest of our day?" She watched him visibly relax.

As Galen had no suggestions, they drove home to Tapestry Court in silence. Finally he looked over toward Elizabeth. "What's wrong, Bits?"

She shook her head. "I'm not sure. The will of course. Why would Hannah change it two days before her death? Why would she give the New York guys half a million apiece when she should have expected to see them again?"

"Maybe to soften the blow of leaving them out of her will?"

Elizabeth nodded. "Maybe. But why change it when she did? And what was the old will? Who benefitted from it?"

"I can try to find out but I'm not sure Andrews will give out that information." He paused. "Unless of course it might throw some light on the murder."

Elizabeth nodded. "That's what I was wondering."

They left the car in the new garage and instead of going straight to the Manor House, they went through the gate to the garden and sat on a bench near the fountain.

"And all this started here." Galen shook his head.

"Well, this didn't have anything to do with the new murder."

"I know. But I was thinking about us and the reason I suggested you coming here on your sabbatical. And now it's our first home together."

Elizabeth put her head on his shoulder. "And it feels so right, doesn't it?"

He nodded and took her hand. "I love you, Bits."

"I love you too, Galen. Always. No matter what." And she hoped he didn't realize she meant even if he wouldn't give her the child she wanted.

***

Back at the library, the two newly appointed trustees of the Hannah Drew Theatre stared at each other in silence.

Glenda shook her head. "God bless Hanley Drew!!! I mean Hannah. Do you know what this means, Brandon?"

He nodded his head. "It means several things. The theatre can become all we've dreamed it would be. And you and I will have enough income to be able to devote full time to running it."

He grinned. "This probably isn't the right time but this time I can't wait." He got down on his knees. "Glenda Taylor, will you marry me?"

She grinned back. "Uh, where is the ring you are supposed to be offering?"

For a few seconds his face fell, then he came back with "I wanted you to choose it."

She chewed on a finger and rolled her eyes to the library ceiling. Finally she took pity on his knees. "Well, okay then."

They laughed as he struggled to stand up. And after he kissed her with another chart worthy kiss, he said, "We are going to have a great marriage and life."

Glenda nodded and kissed his hand. "Yes, we are."

But as they walked to their cars, she wondered if such happiness should come springing forth from the murder of such a generous woman.

***

Ron Lockland and Lisa Coulter walked to their cars together in silence. As Lisa opened her door, Ron finally spoke.

"I'd rather have Hannah than a million dollars." He paused and then continued. "But I never had a chance of having Hannah, not really, not the way I wanted her. That was sweet of her to include me though. Of course she would include you. You were like sisters."

Lisa turned an angry look on him. "But why the Brock family? That Carolyn Brock is, well, she's just a, well, you know."

"She didn't leave it to her, but to Margaret."

"And as soon as Margaret reaches twenty one, she'll get it all from her the way she always gets everything she wants."

Ron perked up. "But what about the theater? That's great news, isn't it?"

Lisa glared again. "But why didn't she put us in charge?"

***

Margaret strained against her seat belt in the back seat to lean toward her parents. "What happened? Why are you both so quiet? What did the will mean?"

Her mother turned back toward her, glared and said through gritted teeth. "It means that you are very rich, my dear, and that Mr. and Mrs. Delaney will be in charge of your money for a very long time and your parents won't have anything to say about it."

Her daddy said in his usual patient voice. "Carolyn, later."

Chapter Twelve

Elizabeth was looking over requests in some letters she'd brought home from Mindy's when the doorbell rang. She wasn't sorry for the interruption; invitations to speak made her nervous. She didn't want to commit to travel; she'd come here on Sabbatical for a year. But she wanted to do what God called her to do. *Please show me Your will, Lord!*

She was glad to see Reggie and Sara there when she opened the door. "Come on in, girls!"

"We want to talk," said Reggie seriously. "Where do you want us?"

"You decide. Here in the parlor" she pointed to her right. "In the library, or in the kitchen along with tea and muffins?"

"Kitchen!" Both girls spoke at the same time and Elizabeth joined in their laughter.

When the tea was ready, blueberry muffins warmed in the microwave, and soft butter in her bluebird butter dish sitting on the table, they all sat down and the girls began buttering muffins.

"Now what do you want to talk about?"

They looked at each other uncomfortably. Then Reggie spoke.

"We don't want to worry Mom so we thought we'd come and talk to you."

Elizabeth nodded encouragement.

Then Sara took over. "Mrs. Delaney, we just don't think what happened to me was an accident. And we wondered if the person who did it thought Judy was Reggie."

Reggie added, "We don't want to sound all dramatic or anything but Sara is remembering more and more and says the driver came way up on the sidewalk, not just a little way - like it was on purpose. And if it really was an accident, surely they wouldn't have run away."

Both girls looked at her and Elizabeth took a deep breath and sent up a quick silent prayer for wisdom.

"I think you girls are very smart. You've thought things out about the accident and Judy's death. But if you are right, why? Why would somebody want to harm you?"

This time the girls looked at each other. And Reggie finally answered.

"Well, we wondered if maybe it had something to do with Ms. Drew's murder."

"Did either or both of you see anything unusual the night of her death?"

They shook their heads. "Not that we can think of," Reggie answered.

"What do you remember?"

Reggie spoke first. "It was almost time for me to go on stage and I had to go to the bathroom."

"And I went with her," Sara added.

"And you saw nothing?"

They both shook their heads.

"And you saw nobody?"

"No." Reggie shook her head again.

Then Sara spoke. "Well, Ms. Coulter was coming out of the bathroom when we got there. But nothing strange about that."

Reggie added. "And they were best friends so she wouldn't have done it."

Elizabeth nodded. "Then I can't see why anyone would want to silence you two. Can you?"

Reggie hesitated before she spoke. "I guess not."

Sara added, "But it seems so weird that the accident that didn't seem like an accident happened the night after the murder."

Elizabeth put down her teacup. "Coincidences do happen."

The girls nodded.

Then Elizabeth added, "But just in case somebody thinks you know something you don't know, be careful."

"Oh, we will, Miss Dail...I mean Mrs. Delaney. I promise." Reggie picked up her cup and drained it.

"No worry about that!" Sara added and finished off her own tea.

As Elizabeth let the girls out of the front door, she hugged them both and said "Please come back again soon."

"We will!" And they waved goodbye.

She wondered how long Sara would be staying with the Tates. And when she went back to where the request letters lay on her desk in the library, somehow she couldn't make herself pick them up again.

There was too much to think about right here, right now.

***

Am I safe or not? I might not have even needed to take all those risks. Evidently not. It's been over two weeks and nothing. I think I can relax now, thanks be to the gods.

***

They were in the library and Galen was reading while she looked over her lists on the computer. But she still couldn't concentrate, and stood up.

She felt all shaky inside but it had to be said. "Are you sure, Galen, that we really can't have a baby?"

He threw down the book he was reading and said through gritted teeth. "Yes I'm sure. NO WAY!" Again the Galen she didn't know was glaring at the floor.

"I just don't understand."

He looked up at her and the anger dissolved. "I'm sorry." Then he dropped his head into his hands and she saw tears fall through his fingers.

She had never seen him in tears before. "What is it, Galen? What's wrong? If you don't want a baby, it's okay. I won't ever push it again, I promise."

It was more than tears. He was now bent over and heaving great sobs. Elizabeth knelt down beside him. "What can I do, Sweetheart?"

He just shook his head and she stayed kneeling beside him with her head resting on his arm.

Gradually, finally, the sobbing grew less and he pulled his handkerchief from his pocket and blew his nose one last time. His arm reached around and hugged Elizabeth to him.

"Thank you, Bits. Could we get some coffee and go out on the patio?"

"Of course, Sweetheart. I'll pour and you go on out."

"And I'll tell you about my ugly past."

"Okay." She noticed her hands were trembling as she poured the coffee into their favorite mugs. When she joined him on the porch, she could see he had complete control of himself.

He even smiled as he took his coffee mug from her. "Are you sure you are ready to hear the truth about your husband?"

She smiled at him with all the love she could muster into her eyes. "Of course. I want to know all about you. Everything."

He drew a deep breath and looked out onto the lawn. "Harold told me I should share with you but I was too ashamed. I see now he was right. I need you to understand. I was a senior in high school and got a girl pregnant. She wanted us to get married but I didn't love her and refused. She had an abortion." He paused.

"I'm sorry." Elizabeth stroked his arm.

"And she died."

"Oh, Galen, I'm so sorry. No wonder you're afraid...but that was from an abortion, not a normal childbirth."

"It gets worse."

Elizabeth was surprised but didn't say anything. "Then in college I did it again - got another girl pregnant. I determined I wasn't going to make that mistake again so I asked her to marry me. She hesitated and talked about giving the baby up for adoption.

"That made me mad and as she was walking away I jerked her around by her arm.

"She glared at me and said that if I ever tried to touch her again, she'd say I raped her. I never saw her after that. But I found out later that she died giving birth to the baby she had promised to let a couple adopt."

They were both quiet for a few seconds. Then he said "It was a girl. And she lived. But I could never find out who adopted her. She'd be around twenty five years old now."

"I'm so sorry, Galen. But I know you've repented over both."

"Yes, that's not the problem. It's that I have gotten two people pregnant and they both died because of it. There is nothing in the world that would make me take a chance on killing you."

"But Galen, it wasn't your fault - not the dying part."

He just shook his head and pulled her close. She decided the wisest thing was to just stay in the embrace and be silent.

But then she thought of something. "Galen you have a child. You have a daughter, out there somewhere. And the laws have changed. I think you could find out who adopted her now. You know the mother's name and the approximate date of birth. Today you can find out these thing."

The look on his face was pure shock. "Find my daughter? But she's a grown woman now."

"That doesn't matter, Sweetheart. I've done enough counseling to know that parents, and knowing the birth parents, are important no matter how old a person grows."

He didn't say anything so she went on. "Could I try to find out? I mean I don't want to go against your wishes but would you give me permission to research it?"

After a moment, he nodded.

"Will you tell me the name of her mother?"

He nodded again. "Brenda Short."

Elizabeth took his hand again. "Lord, this is Your business. If You want us to find Galen's daughter; and if she needs to know him, then guide us to the right solution."

Galan added the "Amen."

***

The next afternoon, the doorbell rang again as Elizabeth was looking over the invitations to speak. She was thrilled at the interruption but feeling guilty toward Mindy who had done so much work organizing her correspondence.

It was Reggie and Sara again.

Elizabeth laughed. "Back for more muffins?"

Both girls smiled but Reggie said, "Mrs. Delaney - see I remembered your new name this time - we still aren't convinced about the accident and we want to talk some more. With you, if you don't mind."

"I don't mind at all." Elizabeth stood back and smiled as the girls went straight to the kitchen.

"It just happens I have some blueberry muffins in the freezer. It won't take long to thaw them in the microwave. Is that okay?"

Sara spoke this time. "Sure. Thank you." And she sat down. And stood up again.

"Can I help you?"

Elizabeth started to say no but then realized the girl needed to feel helpful. "Yes, you sure can." She reached in the freezer and pulled out a freezer bag with eight muffins in it. "Take out as many as you two can eat." She showed them another bag. "See, I have plenty more for us."

After some discussion, the girls took half out of the bag.

"Don't you want any, Mrs. Delaney?"

"No thank you, Sara. I had a late lunch and am not at all hungry. Put those on this plate and in the microwave for about fifty seconds. Then I'll heat the water for tea while you two are buttering your muffins. And you can go ahead and start eating so your mouths won't be full the whole time we're talking."

Both girls laughed and in a minute were slathering butter all over the freshly warmed muffins.

When the water was ready, Elizabeth put tea bags in three cups and joined the girls at the table. "Okay, what's going on?"

The girls looked at each other and then Reggie broke the silence. "We don't like Ms. Coulter. We think she did it."

"Her best friend? And why do you think that?"

Sara answered. "We think she's evil."

"You must have a reason to think that. What is it?"

"Well," Reggie hesitated. "It sounds stupid but it's the way she looks at us. Like she is expecting us to accuse her or something. You know, maybe because we saw her coming out of the bathroom."

Sara was nodding. "It's true. She does look at us funny. We really aren't making it up. And I've watched. She doesn't look at other kids like that."

"Mom says she's rich now because Ms. Drew left her a lot of money. So maybe she killed her for that."

Elizabeth remembered the gasp when the lawyer told them that Lisa Coulter and Ron Lockland had each inherited a million dollars. "I don't think she knew she was going to inherit that money."

Reggie glared. "Well, she did inherit it, so why doesn't she quit teaching school? None of the kids like her."

"I don't know but maybe she likes teaching. Or maybe she will quit after her commitment for this year is over."

Sara was swallowing the last of her second muffin. "I never did like her. I hope she does quit. It would make a lot of kids happy."

Elizabeth said hesitantly, "I wonder why she and Hannah were such good friends? Hannah seemed like such a nice person."

Both girls nodded. And looked at Elizabeth as though they were expecting her to solve the problem.

"I'm sorry I don't have any answers, girls. But I promise you I will check into things. I promise."

Reggie gave a sigh of relief. "Thank you, Mrs. Delaney."

Sara got up, gathered cups and plates and took them to the sink. "Can I wash the dishes?"

Elizabeth started to say no, but again had a check in her heart. "Oh would you, Sara? That would be such a help." And she was rewarded by the smile on the girl's face.

***

Chuck was fed up. Not only did he have to have another girl in the house but now she and Reggie were always going over to Mrs. Delaney's. It used to be his special place.

And he still believed Ms. D liked him best. Hadn't she given him all those ships that belonged to Colonel, well, his grandfather? He'd never known the Colonel but after all he'd heard about him, how he made everybody work hard and thought he was so important, he couldn't imagine him as a grandfather, not the kind you read about in books or saw on TV. But he'd left everything to his son, who turned out to be Chuck's father and that was a good thing.

But Chuck missed Ms. D. He never called her that to her face just first Miss Daily and now Mrs. Delaney. She was like an aunt or something and she was the first adult to call him Chuck instead of Charles. If it hadn't been for her, he'd probably still be Charles to his parents.

He wanted to talk to her about the murder. And about the guy he saw that night sneaking around Tapestry Court. When the girls were safely back home and giggling up in Reggie's bedroom, he went in the kitchen. "Mom, I'm going out." And before she could warn him, he continued. "And I won't go outside the Court I promise."

When he got to the Manor House, he rang the doorbell and Elizabeth Delaney opened it almost immediately. He knew she wasn't faking the happiness on her face when she saw him.

"Chuck! Come in. I've missed you."

"I've missed you too, Ms. D." He gulped. "I mean Mrs. Delaney."

"You know, I kind of like you calling me Ms. D."

"You do?" He was shocked.

She laughed. "Yes I do. I really do."

She headed toward the kitchen. "Want some hot chocolate?"

"Yes Ma'am."

"And a couple of muffins?"

"Yes Ma'am. But mostly I want to talk."

"You've got all three. Have a seat."

When they were seated at the table with microwaved muffins and cups of hot chocolate, Elizabeth asked. "So what do you want to talk about, young Chuck?"

He looked at her seriously. "Murder."

She nodded.

"I know we're safe now but I keep thinking I should tell somebody about that guy I saw sneaking around here at the court before they got the garage and locks all back up."

"You may be right, Chuck. I was thinking about talking to Deputy Collins about some things. If I can get him to come over some day after school, would you want to tell him?"

"Yes! I really think I'd feel better if the law officers knew about it."

"Okay, excuse me a minute and I'll try to call him." She left the kitchen and went toward the library and the house phone. He wondered why she didn't use her cell phone.

When she came back she was smiling. "He will be here tomorrow around four. Is that okay with you?"

He nodded enthusiastically. "Thank you, Ms. D. I'll feel so much better after I tell him." Then he paused. "And Ms. D., I found this near the side of our front porch. You know, the next day after the night I saw the guy. I don't know if it means anything but I picked it up and... Well, I felt a little silly but thought I'd better bring it to show you."

Elizabeth took the paper he handed her. "Thank you, Chuck. We'll see if it's important."

He went home feeling like the expression "a happy camper" though he wasn't sure what that meant.

***

Elizabeth stared at the paper in her hand. Of course if she turned it upside down, it might not mean what she originally thought. She looked at her watch. She had nearly an hour before Galen would be home so she grabbed her sweater and left by the front door, being sure to lock it. And that irritated her. Surely Tapestry Court was safe again.

Harold Fowler opened the door himself. He greeted Elizabeth enthusiastically as usual and explained that Lucy had gone to Lexington to visit her sister, Lydia; Mindy Simmons took her. And he added with a grin, "Lydia and Lucy giggle a lot these days, like they are both getting younger. It looks like there may be more wedding bells in the near future."

"Stephen Richardson?"

Harold nodded with a big smile on his face.

"Oh! I'm so glad. Is his leg healed?" The nice man was temporarily in the nursing home where Lydia Tapestry had been for a long time. He had hurt his leg and didn't expect to be there long. And with the breakthrough in Lydia's repressed trauma, she had blossomed like a rose that had been a bud for a long, long time. The two were obviously in love and Elizabeth was happy for them.

"Yes, he plans to leave next week and go home. But he swears he's not leaving her behind." The minister grinned. "So, I may have another wedding to perform soon."

"That's wonderful, Harold. Things worked out so well, didn't they? For everybody. Mindy and Charles are going to have a baby, Joel and Jenny are so in love, George is the acknowledged heir and head of Tapestry Industries. And ..."

"And you and Galen are happy?" There was a slight question in his voice.

"Yes, Harold, we are. Galen told me he came to talk to you about his past. And he finally told me. We're not telling anyone but I'm going to try to find the child that was adopted."

"Is that a good idea?"

"We won't approach her unless it seems right. So please add your prayers to ours."

He nodded. "I'm glad." He turned toward the kitchen. "I'd offer you something but I'm not sure what Lucy has..."

"I really don't want anything. Can we go to your office and talk?"

"Sure." And she followed him in.

"I need your opinion. Not only have you been a pastor but you were overseas and I thought you might know something about witchcraft."

Harold Fowler laughed. "Well! It's not often that someone blindsides me, but I sure didn't expect that one. I'm certainly not an expert but I'll try to answer your questions.

She reached in her pocket and pulled out the paper Chuck gave her. When he took it, he nodded.

"Upside down pentagram. Sign of the devil."

"That's what I thought. But if you turn the paper the other way, it's just a regular star."

"Where did you get it?"

"I hope I'm not betraying Chuck's trust but he's going to talk to Deputy Collins tomorrow after school so I think it's okay. I wanted to have the facts straight before we met with him." And she told him about Chuck seeing the stranger at Tapestry Court and finding the paper beside their front porch.

Harold Fowler surprised her by saying, "I'm not surprised. From the beginning of the summer, when Reggie asked for prayer to get the part she wanted in the play, I've had a definite awareness of evil and danger. And it wasn't for that Ms. Drew. It was for Reggie. And now I think the girl that's staying with them too."

Elizabeth nodded. "Has anybody talked to you about the 'accident'?"

He nodded. "Yes, Linda came over for prayer and told me about the candy too."

"Good. There's no question there's a big problem but I can't see how the girls are involved. They don't remember seeing anything unusual around the time of the murder."

"Well somebody has it in for them. And Elizabeth, this symbol. You said it was normal if you turn it upside down. But normal people don't carry around a piece of black paper with a red pentagram. This is definitely a satanic symbol. And it was probably left on purpose at the Tate's house with curses on it."

Elizabeth stared with horror at the paper lying on Harold Fowler's desk. "Curses?"

"You wouldn't believe - nor would most Christians - how many curses are pronounced against churches, people, and nations. Satan worshippers and witches are more aware of the power in words than the Body of Christ is." He shook his head. "Even though the Bible is full of wisdom like 'The power of life and death is in the tongue.' Don't ever forget that, Elizabeth, Proverbs 18:21."

She got up and went to hug Harold Fowler. "Would you pray now? And, uh, do you mind putting that paper in an envelope so I don't have to touch it again?"

"Of course. And of course not." He stood up and placed the paper in an envelope he pulled from drawer of the desk. Then he took her hand. "Father we stand here before Your throne, hand in hand, and we thank you that by the Blood of Jesus, You wash away all curses from us, from young Charles, uh Chuck, and from the Tate household, all of Tapestry Court and from anyone else this paper may contact, like the Deputy. We dissolve those curses to be completely ineffective. Especially, Lord, we hold up Reggie and her friend who seem to be under attack from the evil one and we declare protection over them. No weapon formed against them will prosper. And Lord, we are asking You to expose the murderer of Hannah Drew. In Jesus Name we pray. Amen."

"Amen," Elizabeth echoed. And picked up the envelope.

Chapter Thirteen

Elizabeth hung up the phone in a state of shock. Brenda Short gave her baby up for adoption to Ann and Thomas Crossfield. She'd have to find out if they were who she thought they were. She picked back up the phone and in a short time Linda answered.

"Hey, can I come visit or would we have any privacy?"

"Yes, remember, the kids are back in school."

Elizabeth breathed a sigh of relief. She was so shaken, it had temporarily escaped her memory. "Be right there."

When the two friends were settled at the Tate's kitchen table with coffee cups, and Linda's homemade apple dumplings as a temptation in between them, Linda spoke first.

"Okay, let's have it."

"Well you know about the baby issue."

Linda nodded.

"I've found out something. I'm not going to tell you the whole story but I need some information that you have and if it's right, I'll tell you part of it."

Linda nodded. "Okay."

"What was Jenny Anderson's mother's name?"

Linda looked surprised at the question but quickly answered. "Ann."

She looked even more surprised when all the color drained from Elizabeth's face.

"And her father was Thomas Crossfield?"

"Yes."

"Oh, Linda. One more question. Was Jenny adopted?"

"I wasn't here at the time but yes, George told me that they couldn't have children so they adopted a little girl. He said it was kind of a sad situation. They had agreed on the adoption before the child was born and all the papers had been signed, which was good since the mother died giving birth."

Elizabeth took a deep breath. "Are you ready for a surprise?"

"I'm sitting down."

"I feel guilty telling you this first but...Galen is Jenny's biological father."

Linda's mouth dropped open. After a few seconds she said, "I'm speechless."

"This is one of the things he had against me getting pregnant. He was afraid I would die giving birth."

Linda nodded. "That's understandable but..."

"Does Jenny know she's adopted? Or does she think they were her biological parents?"

"I don't know. Isn't that awful. She's wanted to be closer to me and I don't even know that. Do you want me to ask her?"

Elizabeth was silent a moment before she spoke. "No, you know I counseled her a few months ago. I think I can find out by talking to her. And if she knows, I'll let Galen decide how - and if - to let her know."

What a day. The shock of finding out who Galan's daughter is, and then in a few minutes Deputy Collins and Chuck would be here. Elizabeth didn't think there would be time to talk to Jenny before Galen got home but she sure wanted to.

Just then her cell phone rang. It was Galen. "Bits, I'm kind of tied up at the bank. Do you mind if I just drive through and get something for supper and be home around 8:30 or 9?"

She tried to keep her voice from showing the relief and gladness she felt at the extra time. "Of course not. But I'll be glad to see you when you get here. Love you so much."

"I love you too. Kiss your nose for me, Bits."

She grinned as she turned off the phone. She loved their private jokes. Okay, now... And then the buzzer that was installed in the kitchen went off. She spoke into the speaker "Deputy Collins?"

The reply came immediately. "Yes Ma'am." So she pushed the button that would unlock the gate from the garage to the Tapestry Court Park. "Come on in. You know which is my house? The first one here at this end."

"Yes Ma'am, I'll be right there."

Within minutes the front doorbell rang and there were two males on her doorstep, the Deputy and Chuck Tate.

When they were seated around the table with the rest of the thawed blueberry muffins, Chuck's hot chocolate, Deputy Collins' coffee, and Elizabeth's tea, the Deputy opened the conversation.

"So what's all this about?" He looked at Chuck. "Miz Delaney said you wanted to talk to me."

So Chuck told him about looking out the window in the middle of the night and seeing a person sneaking around toward the garage which was torn down and left the gated community exposed to the world. "I'm sorry I didn't tell anybody but Ms. D earlier, but I wasn't sure if it was a big deal or just somebody curious."

Elizabeth took over the conversation. "And there is another thing, Deputy. Chuck found this in their yard. He didn't think anything about it at first but brought it to me yesterday." She handed him the envelope. "It wasn't in an envelope then, just on the ground."

Deputy Collins opened the envelope and took out the black paper with the red star on it. He looked at Elizabeth with a question in his eyes.

"That is a satanic symbol." She looked over at Chuck.

A "Whoa!" exploded from Chuck's mouth.

The Deputy looked uncomfortable for at least a minute and then said, "Miz Delaney." He cleared his throat "There's some information I was going to give you but..." . And looked at Chuck.

Elizabeth smiled at the boy. "I trust Chuck implicitly but I understand. Chuck, do you think that now since you've shared what you saw and given what you found, you could leave us to talk alone?"

It was obvious that Chuck was not happy about having to leave. But he stood up and wiped the last muffin crumb from his lips. "Sure. I understand." Then he looked at the Deputy. "But as soon as everything is solved, I want to be one of the first to know. Okay?"

"Okay." The Deputy gave him a salute and Chuck saluted back and left them.

When they heard the front door close, Elizabeth looked eagerly at the Deputy for the news and he shared.

"There were some things we found at the murder site that haven't been made public. It seems strange but what the boy found confirms what it seemed to indicate. First there were some blood spots on the doorsill of the dressing room in the form of upside down crosses. And then there was a knife, with a white handle in the trash can of the women's restroom. It had been wiped clean of blood and fingerprints. But there was enough blood left where the blade joins the handle to prove that it was the victim's blood."

"But what does that have to do with the paper Chuck found?"

"We found out from an expert in the State Police that the knife with a white handle is used in satanic or witch-craft rituals."

Elizabeth let out a huge sigh. "Oh dear. But who on earth in the list of suspects would be involved in witch-craft or satanism?"

"I don't know, Ma'am. But I'm sure hoping you find out." Then he grinned. "Remember that two hundred and fifty dollars apiece!"

Elizabeth walked the Deputy through the garden and to the visitors section of the new garage, opening the gate with her special password. The officer was very impressed with the new system, a password for each resident and an audio and button control in each home.

After they said goodbye and promised to stay in touch, Elizabeth walked through the garden and to Jenny Anderson's back door.

There was surprise and a smile on the young lady's face when she saw who was there. "Elizabeth! Come in."

Elizabeth shook her head. "No, I came to invite you to visit me at the Manor House."

Jenny frowned.

"I know," Elizabeth said softly. "But I think it's time. And I want to talk to you."

"Okay." Jenny grabbed a sweater from a hook beside the back door.

"Thank you so much, Mrs. Delaney." Jenny Anderson looked around Elizabeth's kitchen . "This is the first time I've been here since...well you know. And I don't feel all creepy." She smiled a sweet smile at Elizabeth.

"I'm so glad, Jenny." She refilled their teacups with the orange spice tea and offered Jenny another scone. "Tell me about your parents."

"That's interesting that you say that. I've been thinking about them a lot. You remember that I blamed the Colonel for keeping them busy and that's why they never came to any of my school productions or anything like that. But I don't think that was all the story. I really don't think they liked being parents. Well at least not to me." Jenny took a sip of tea. "Don't get me wrong; I'm not angry at them. But

I knew I needed to forgive Colonel Tapestry for everything so I thought about that a lot. If they - or at least Mother - had wanted to be with me, she could have told the Colonel she had other things to do."

Elizabeth nodded.

"And then when they sent me off to boarding school, Mother told me something. I've never talked about it but she told me I was adopted. And since then I thought I must have been a big disappointment or something. I didn't get to talk it over with them because they died too soon, you know while I was too young to know how to ask them."

She shrugged and made a sad little smile. "I've wondered who my real parents are but don't even know how to find out. All those things are why I've spent most of my life since school just watching movies. Escaping from thinking about all that."

Elizabeth got up and went over and hugged Jenny. "You have really had a tough life, haven't you?"

Jenny gave a little laugh. "I guess so. Poor me, huh?"

"Can I pray for you?"

"Sure."

"I mean here, now."

She saw Jenny swallow with difficulty. "I think I ought to tell you something else. I forgave the Colonel and I forgave Mother and Father. I even forgave my birth parents who gave me away. But..."

Elizabeth waited.

"But I can't seem to forgive God for letting all the awful things happen to me." Then the tears started.

Elizabeth took her hand. "Dear heavenly Father, You are Love, and I am so aware of Your love for your precious little girl Jenny. I'm asking you to show her that when all the bad things happened to her, You had a plan to redeem them and work all things to her good. You never cause bad things - fallen people do. But You are Love and have a way to bring joy, peace and love to us when we look to

You. Help Jenny see you for who you really are. I ask it in Jesus' Name."

There was silence for a few minutes except for a few sniffs from Jenny who reached for a tissue from the box Elizabeth had put on the table.

Finally Jenny spoke. "God, I know Jesus saved me from hell, but I don't really know You as Father. I never had a real one so please forgive me for blaming You for things that happen in this world that aren't Your fault. And I know You always forgive so I thank You. In Jesus Name, Amen." Then she looked up at Elizabeth with a smile that seemed to glow out from her very heart.

It seemed forever 'til Galen got home even though it was before 8:30 when he walked in the kitchen door.

"Oh Galen, I'm so glad to see you!"

He pulled her to him. "And as always I am glad to see you, Mrs. Delaney!" Then he backed up and looked her in the face. "Are you okay?"

She nodded. "Yes but it's been quite a day."

"Tell me."

"Can we go in the library?"

"Sure."

As soon as they were settled, she said, "Okay, Galen, you are in for a shock." She took his hand.

"You found her? You found my daughter?"

Elizabeth nodded.

"Have you talked to her?"

"Sort of."

"What do you mean? Does she know that I am her father?"

"No. She knows nothing except she was adopted and she has forgiven her adoptive parents for an unloving upbringing and forgiven her biological parents for giving her up." Elizabeth smiled. "And she forgave God for being mad at Him over it all."

"Well you had quite a conversation with a stranger!"

"Galen, this is the big shock. She's not a stranger."

He pulled his hand away from hers, not in anger but to raise both hands in the air in a questioning gesture.

"Galen, she doesn't know it. It's up to you whether to let her know or not. But your daughter is Jenny Anderson, Jenny Crossfield Anderson. Brenda Short signed the adoption papers giving her child to Thomas and Ann Crossfield before she died giving birth to a daughter. The Crossfields named her Jennifer."

There was a long silence that Elizabeth did not want to interrupt.

He finally spoke. "Do you think she would want to know? You said she's forgiven us for giving her up but would she want to know me?"

"Galen, one of the things when we were talking that she prayed hurt my heart. She asked God to forgive her for blaming Him, that she never had a real Father and couldn't understand what being a father meant."

There was another long silence. "Bits, what about you? If we let her know and begin a relationship, it would change our lives."

"Sweetheart, it would change our lives for the better. It might be a shock at first but honestly I think she would have an empty place filled to know you want a relationship with her."

He stood up. "How soon can we tell her?'

Elizabeth grinned. "Want me to call her now and see if we can visit?"

He looked at his watch. "Yes, I'm sure they are still up."

Jenny was thrilled at the request for an invitation. "I've made some pecan pie and we haven't eaten dessert yet. We would love to have you and Mr. Delaney join us."

Elizabeth was glad Jenny couldn't see the grin on her face. *Mr. Delaney! Not for long.*

"I don't think I can eat any pecan pie," Galen confessed nervously as they made their way to Number Three, Tapestry Court, their closest neighbors to the left.

"Maybe you can later. I'll ask if we can go in the living room first and have a talk."

He nodded. "Good."

Joel and Jenny both greeted them with obvious pleasure and then Elizabeth said, "Could we wait on the pecan pie and just sit in here and have a talk for a few minutes?"

"Sure," Joel said and picked up his jacket from the couch and took it to the closet. Then he sat down in what was obviously his favorite recliner and Jenny sat in the one beside him.

Elizabeth said. "This may come as a shock. But I hope it will be a nice surprise."

The young couple looked at her expectantly.

"Galen has something he wants to tell you, Jenny."

Galen looked over at Jenny Anderson with both fear and hope in his eyes.

"Jenny, I know you know you were adopted but don't know if you know anything about your birth mother."

Jenny swallowed. "No, Sir. Well, I know she died when I was born. And that made me feel guilty. If it weren't for me, she would still be alive."

"No, if it weren't for me, she would still be alive."

"What do you mean?"

"Jenny." He paused and swallowed. "Jenny, I am your daddy."

Her eyes widened and nobody said a word.

Then Galen started speaking again. "I asked your mother, whose name was Brenda, to marry me when we found out she was pregnant but, well, we hadn't been in love and she said "No." I never saw her again. And I was ashamed. I should have kept in touch and adopted you myself. And I'm asking you to forgive me."

And then to everyone's shock, Jenny lowered her recliner and walked over to the couch. She knelt before Galen and looked up into his eyes as tears fell from her own.

"My daddy? You said you are my daddy? Not just my father but my daddy?"

"Oh Sweetheart," and Galen reached down and wrapped her in his arms. "Yes, yes. I am your daddy. And I'll be as much of a daddy as you'll let me be. I've longed for my child. And here you are."

Through her tears Jenny backed up, looked at him, and gave a laugh. "And we live next door to each other. Oh, Daddy. Isn't God good?"

Then the room was filled with tears and laughter and hugs until the two couples held hands and Galen led them in a prayer of thanksgiving and praise.

After that the most tasty pecan pie in the world was enjoyed by all.

Elizabeth and Galen walked home slowly in the moonlight, holding hands. They went through the Manor House gate and he got out his key and unlocked the door. As soon as they were inside, he put his hand out and stopped her.

"Thank you," he said.

"No need to thank me. It was no trouble. I just made a few calls and some of my former colleagues helped me."

"No, I don't mean just for that. I mean for forgiving me for what a jerk I was over the whole baby issue. And, I really mean this, for wanting to have my baby in the first place. And for bringing up the subject. If you hadn't, my desire for my daughter would have never been fulfilled."

"You are welcome, Galen. I still don't know how I feel about having my own baby. But now at least I have a stepdaughter. And..."

"And?"

She pulled away and started up the steps. "I don't know. We'll see." Then she stopped and turned toward him. "Oh! I forgot to tell you the other big news."

He switched on the stairway light and turned off the porch and entrance hall lights. "Other big news?"

"Come on upstairs and I'll tell you while we're getting ready for bed."

Galen grinned. "I'm ready now, my new bride."

She shook her head and continued up the steps. And then she started talking when they were in the bedroom.

"Witchcraft? Satanism? What on earth?"

Elizabeth shrugged. "It's a shame those New York guys had already gone and couldn't have dropped that picture. I just can't imagine anybody around here being involved in a coven or whatever they call it."

"I've heard stuff like that goes on, but Simpsonton doesn't seem to be a good setting for that kind of thing."

"I know." Elizabeth pulled the covers down and got in. "Well, have we had enough drama for tonight?"

He smiled down at her. "Well, maybe we could have a different kind?'

Her eyes twinkled. "Maybe."

Chapter Fourteen

Harold Fowler watched as Lucy set the phone down. He didn't know when he'd ever seen her so excited.

"They are definitely coming!"

He breathed a sigh of relief. She would have been so disappointed if they weren't. It had been nearly two years since they'd seen their son, Jackson, or their grandsons, and of course their lovely daughter-in-law. They would only be able to stay for two days but... *Thank you, Lord.*

"Oh, I need to call Elizabeth and see if Lydia and Richard can stay in the guest cottage next Friday night after the wedding. At their age, they don't need to be driving after the reception. They wouldn't have any energy left..." She stopped and blushed. "I mean..."

He grinned at her. "I know what you mean. And that's a good idea to call Elizabeth."

She picked up the phone again and he interrupted her. "Why don't you invite her down for tea or something and ask her during the visit. I haven't seen her much lately. She's a nice lady"

Lucy nodded. "Yes she is and I miss her too."

Within a few minutes the three were seated in the kitchen with herb tea for the two ladies and coffee for Harold.

"We have a favor to ask," Lucy said with a big smile on her face.

"I'm sure the answer will be yes." Elizabeth smiled back.

"Well it's about the wedding night. We wondered if Lydia and Stephen could stay in your guest house."

Elizabeth laughed. "It's not my guesthouse. It belongs to George. Well, I guess it goes along with the rent for the Manor House. Of course!" She grimaced. "But since Galen and I got married and nobody has stayed there I haven't cleaned it. I'll need to get busy."

Lucy shook her head. "I know Hattie would love to do it. You know, make her feel a part of things."

"I agree." Elizabeth felt a little guilty that she hadn't made any effort to spend time with Hattie who had lived alone since Emily Caine died. "Why don't I go by and visit her when I leave here and ask her myself?" She paused a minute. "Should I offer to pay her?"

"Absolutely not." Harold shook his head. "It would feel insulting to her. She's part of the Tapestry Court family."

"That's what I thought but wasn't sure."

Lucy seemed bursting at the seams with excitement. "And guess what? Our son and his family are coming for the wedding! We will get to see them in just a week. Isn't that awesome?"

"Oh, I'm so happy for you." And Elizabeth meant it. Of course she had her own excitement but Galen and Jenny had decided to wait until after Lydia Tapestry's wedding to make their own news public.

"Elizabeth," Harold's voice became more serious. "Have you found out anything more about the murder?"

She glanced over at Lucy.

"It's okay," he said. "She knows everything I know."

Elizabeth nodded. "It seems that some more satanic or witchcraft evidence was found at the high school - you know, the scene of the crime."

Harold shook his head. "I just can't imagine." Then he reached out and took the hands of his wife and Elizabeth. "Father, please give everyone wisdom to solve this thing and root out witchcraft from among us. And stop any danger to anyone else. In Jesus' Name we ask it. Amen." And he let go of their hands.

"Thank you," Elizabeth said and stood up. "I guess I'll go visit Hattie now. And I'll call as soon as I get home." She headed toward the door and then turned around. "Thank you for the tea and the company. I'm so glad about all your family good news."

The couple stood at the door smiling as she walked up the walk toward Number Two.

Hattie Griffin seemed thrilled to see her when she opened the door. "Why Miz Delaney, come on in!"

Elizabeth reached out and hugged the older woman. "I want to apologize for not coming to visit you sooner, Hattie. And please, please just call me Elizabeth."

Hattie frowned. "That don't seem proper."

"But it is. We're friends and I call you Hattie."

The older lady grinned and nodded. "Okay, Elizabeth. Have a seat." And she pointed to the couch that was very much like the one in the Manor House parlor.

Elizabeth sat down. "I especially feel bad because I'm coming to ask you a favor."

"Well, praise the Lord!" Hattie threw her arms up in the air.

Elizabeth was puzzled and obviously Hattie noticed.

"Miz, I mean Elizabeth, ever since Miz Emily died it seems like nobody needs me. Everybody I usually see's been so busy with that play and then the murder and that hurt child. I prayed about being able to do something for somebody."

Elizabeth laughed. "Well I guess I'm the answer to your prayer. You know about Lydia Tapestry getting married?"

Hattie nodded. "And going to be married here in the Court, just like you and Mr. Delaney."

"Yes. Well, Lucy Fowler and I think it would be nice if they could spend their honeymoon night in the guest house but I haven't cleaned it since my own wedding."

"Yes Ma'am! I would love to clean it."

Elizabeth smiled at the enthusiasm on Hattie's face. "Well you have a week. The wedding is a week from tomorrow, that Friday night. And right before I got to the Fowlers they found out their son and his family are coming in for the wedding and will stay with Harold and Lucy. They will come in on Thursday and fly back on Saturday."

"My, my. Isn't this a wonderful thing?"

"Yes, it is. Lydia Tapestry is such a nice lady and I'm so glad she's well now. And I got to meet Stephen Richardson too. He seems like a wonderful man."

"I'm glad. But Miz...I mean Elizabeth, I don't have a good feeling about this murder thing. I wish they'd catch whoever did it. Seems like it's hanging over all our heads, making a shadow even on the good things."

"I agree, Hattie. Tell you what. You pray very well, why don't you pray that the truth comes out? And soon!"

"Yes, Ma'am. You got it!"

When Elizabeth reached the door, she said. "I'd love to visit with you again. And please come over to my place any time."

Hattie grinned. "I'd like that. I used to clean it too. When Miz Emily'd let me. She liked to do it herself but she got so she couldn't do the hard stuff. It's such a pretty house."

Elizabeth smiled happily. "Yes, it is. It's the prettiest home I've ever had." She turned back as she exited the door. "You have the key to the guest house?"

"Sure do. Don't waste your thoughts on it again."

"But I think I'd like us to place some fresh flowers in the bedroom."

"Good idea, Miz...uh, I mean Elizabeth!"

Elizabeth nodded. "I'll order them."

***

Linda Tate was getting nervous. Hers was the only car left in the parents pick up lane in front of the high school. She was about to get out and go in when Reggie and Sara walked out the front door and she breathed a sigh of relief.

"What took you so long?" she asked as soon as Reggie opened the passenger side door. Sara was climbing in the back seat, but was the first to answer.

"That woman, Mrs. Coulter. She had us stay after class to ask what we thought about the murder. If we had any idea who did it. Isn't that weird?"

Linda hesitated only for a few seconds. "Yes, it is. Very strange. I mean, for a teacher. But maybe she doesn't have anyone else to talk to about it."

Reggie spoke up. "And she told us she missed seeing us since we saw so much of each other during the play. Then she asked if we were going to audition for the Christmas show."

Sara added, "And she said she hoped we would."

Reggie said. "I want to, but I really don't want to be around her."

Linda didn't say anything as they drove back to Tapestry Court in silence. But her mind was racing with thoughts about the discussion she and George had just last night about private Christian school for Reggie and Chuck. But what about Sara? They were the closest thing to family she had, and Reggie was her only friend. But tuition for three? Even with their greatly increased income, they might need to pray a lot about this. And would the kids object?

***

"Have you contacted Gilbert Andrews yet about Hannah Drew's old will?" Elizabeth waited until she and Galen had washed the dishes and were settled comfortably in the library.

He slapped his hand on the arm of the leather couch. "No! I'm sorry, Bits. It completely slipped my mind. We have so much going on at work, I just forgot. Why don't you call him?"

"I thought it would look more official coming from you. If I call, it would just seem like curiosity."

"But we're both trustees over Margaret's inheritance."

"I know. But... what excuse can I give?"

There was a short pause before he said "Well, just tell him we were curious if Margaret was included in the previous will, or just added after Hannah met the child."

Elizabeth nodded. "Okay. That sounds reasonable. And if he says he can't tell us, that's that."'

"I just don't want you to get yourself in any danger, Elizabeth." The stern Galen voice was back.

And it almost made Elizabeth giggle. She restrained herself from saying 'You're Jenny's daddy, not mine.' Instead she said, "I won't. I promise."

Galen just looked at her and then turned the television on.

She sighed.

"What's wrong?"

"Oh nothing really. It's just that it's Friday night and I'll have to wait 'til Monday morning to call him." Then she added, "Oh, I almost forgot. Hattie is going to clean the guest house. I told the Fowlers that Lydia and Richard could spend their wedding night there. I hope you don't mind. And I need to call the florist in the morning to have flowers delivered here next Friday during the day so we can put them in the bedroom of the guest house." She reached for a notebook and pen to add the call to her list. And add the call to the attorney to her list for Monday.

"Of course not." After a few seconds passed, he hit the control and turned off the TV. "Bits, I want to ask you something."

She looked over with a question mark in her eyes and scooted closer to him on the couch.

"It's about this house, and the guest house too, I guess. I mean. I was wondering. Would you want to live here permanently?"

Elizabeth felt her heart speed up with excitement. "Why? I mean why do you ask?"

"Answer me first."

"The answer is a definite 'yes' but there's a definite 'but' that goes along with that. BUT I don't want you commuting like you've had to."

He nodded. "Well, one of the reasons we are so busy at work is something that came out of my trip. There is a good possibility that my bank will shortly own and take over the local bank here in Simpsonton."

She sat up and stared.

"And if that happens, and I'm pretty sure it will, I could probably get the presidency of this branch."

"What about the man who's now president of the Simpsonton Bank?"

"He's ready to retire anyway. And said he'll stay and help the transition if we buy it."

"Oh Galen! Would you want to do that?" It would mean giving up his home in Lexington.

"Truthfully? Yes. Not a qualm about leaving Lexington. I think I feel more at home here than I ever felt in my life. And now there's Jenny." He grinned. "But, what about your practice? You just took a sabbatical. Don't you want to return next year?"

Elizabeth didn't say what she was really thinking. "I can open a new practice here if I want, rent an office down town."

He nodded. "Then you want me to definitely put in for the position? They've hinted since they know I'm living here until next spring."

"Yes, oh, yes, Galen." She snuggled up against him with her head on his shoulder.

"There's just one thing."

She glanced up and saw that his face as serious as his voice.

"I would want to sell my house and buy here. I don't want to waste money on renting. Do you think George would sell the Manor House?"

"Well, he and Linda don't want it." Then she thought of Chuck. And Reggie. "But they may want their children to have it someday. I don't know, Galen. Are you going to ask him?"

He nodded. "Now that I've got the 'go ahead' from you!"

***

The next afternoon, Galen called George Tate and asked if he was busy that Saturday with his family or if he would have time to go into town for coffee, just the two of them. George agreed and the two met in the newly remodeled garage where Galen already had his own car started.

He drove them to a local restaurant called Milward's which specialized in great desserts. "If it's okay, I thought we might indulge in a piece of pie or something with our coffee."

George grinned. "Always okay with me to indulge."

It was an old fashioned kind of place with white linen tablecloths and candles in the center of the tables. After they were seated, George with a piece of coconut cream pie, and Galen with pecan, George looked at Galen. "Okay, what's up?"

Galen crunched through a few pecans and swallowed the bite he had just put in his mouth. "I'll just come right out with it. Are you at all willing to sell the Manor House?"

George looked surprised but then thoughtful. "I'll have to check with Linda. She and I don't want to live there but I don't know if she thinks it should be part of the kid's inheritance or something."

Galen nodded. "That's what Elizabeth said. But we both would like to live there permanently." Then he told his friend about the possibility of the career move.

He could tell George was pleased. "I can't think of anything I'd like more than for you and Elizabeth to stay here. The whole court feels like you are family."

Galen choked, coughed a few seconds, took a drink of water and then said, "Yes, we feel the same way." After a short pause, during which he reminded himself that his own news was going to wait until after the wedding which would be in less than a week, he continued. "This has been quite an eventful few months since Elizabeth came here, hasn't it?"

"Has it ever!!!"

Brushing the crumbs off of his shirt front, Galen said, "Well, see what Linda says and if it's okay, first thing Monday I'm going to ask for that transfer."

"I'll let you know by Sunday night."

Galen nodded.

***

That poisoned candy was probably the stupidest thing I've ever done. Besides killing the wrong girl. They don't know I went to Tapestry Court to finish the job but it should have come out about the candy. Nothing more has been said; it's like the investigation has been dropped. And maybe it has. If so, the gods have watched over me very well. Except that Plutus fell down on his job. Big time.

***

Chuck sat on the edge of his bed with his head in his hands. He wanted to solve the murder but he didn't have a clue where to start. Who in Simpsonton could possibly be mixed up in witchcraft? It seemed like something so weird that couldn't happen around here.

Then he sat up straight. Monday he'd ask the kids at school. Surely some of them would have heard if there was witchcraft or satanic things in their town.

He knew he'd cheated. When Miz D asked him to leave, he didn't. He opened and shut the front door and listened while Deputy Collins told her about the witchcraft stuff at the high school, before he slipped out. But he wasn't sorry he'd cheated. He didn't lie or anything. And he knew things he needed to know. And deserved to know. After all he was the one who saw the intruder and found the witch-craft thing there in the Court.

High School. Hmmm. Maybe he ought to get Reggie in-volved. But then she'd take all the credit for solving the mystery. There was always Sara, but she'd already been hurt enough. He didn't want to ask her to do anything dangerous.

Ah, he knew what he'd do!

***

Elizabeth invited Jenny and Joel Anderson for lunch after church on Sunday. Galan cooked chicken on the grill outside with Jenny watching every move he made, leaving Elizabeth and Joel to celebrate the joy each of their spous-es were feeling.

"Jenny can hardly stand to wait until next Saturday to tell the court. I've never seen her so excited." Then he hung his head. "Not even about me!" Then he looked up and laughed. "Just kidding. She's like a different person, seriously. It's given her something about her self image that she's never had. It's even made a bigger change than the healing over the Tapestry ... well, you know." He grit-ted his teeth when he mentioned the past and then took a deep breath and smiled again.

Elizabeth understood, both from her perspective as a psychologist, and as one who was raised outside a loving family home.

"How are we going to make the announcement?" She had an idea but wasn't sure if it would suit the young couple.

"I don't know. And Jenny doesn't either. Maybe go house to house?"

"I found out that the Fowler's son and his family fly out at one thirty that Saturday afternoon so they'd need to leave the court around eleven. I was thinking maybe we could have a small brunch around nine here at our home just for the court families and the newlyweds if they want to get up that early - which they may in order to say good-bye to her nephew and his family. We could make the announcement then. What do you think?"

"I think that would be wonderful - and I know Jenny would love to cook some of the brunch stuff." He smiled.

"I agree. And I would love that too." She glanced out the back window. "Here they come with the chicken. Let's get the rest of the lunch on the table." Elizabeth spooned the potatoes, green beans, and corn into bowls and Joel put them on the table, where the salad bowl already sat awaiting the rest of the meal.

***

"It isn't really stealing," Chuck told himself as he removed his sister's English book from her backpack and put it in his own. He knew it was her last class and so it wouldn't be messing her up if she didn't get it back 'til lunch time. He congratulated himself on finding out all the information he needed to carry out his plan. It sure was good that the middle school and high school were right next door to each other. It wouldn't be any problem at all.

While everyone was at lunch, Chuck excused himself to 'go to the restroom' and hurriedly ran out the side door of the building to the high school. He went boldly in the front door but since no one could be seen at the desk, he marched straight up the steps and peered in the door of the room he'd found out belonged to Ms. Coulter. And breathed a sigh of relief. Nobody there, just as he'd hoped.

But his relief was short lived. Every drawer in the teacher's desk was locked. He was almost back to the door when it opened and Ms. Coulter walked in. She glared at him. "What are you doing here, young man?"

"Uh, uh, looking for my sister." He held up the book. "I found this in my backpack and figured she'd need it."

"Why were you looking for her in my room? I teach Science, not English."

He shrugged his shoulders. "I didn't know what you taught. It just..." Ah! He thought of a good idea. "Yours was the only name I recognized on the doors."

Her face relaxed a little. And so did his insides.

"I think you'll find Reggie in the lunch room." She moved away from in front of the door and his heart stopped pounding so hard.

"Thank you, Ma'am. I'll take it to her now." He made himself smile. And got out of there as fast as he could.

It was almost as bad giving Reggie back the book. She glared as much as Ms. Coulter. "How could this have gotten in your backpack?"

He shrugged. "They were hanging on the hooks next to each other." Then he turned. "I gotta go so I won't get in trouble. See ya."

He slipped back in the middle school door. It had been easier than he thought but zero successful.

***

Elizabeth was put through immediately to Gilbert Andrews' office phone.

"Hello, Mr. Andrews, this is Elizabeth Delaney. Well, I guess you knew that. Your secretary asked my name."

"Yes, Mrs. Delaney. How can I help you?"

"I know we'll have other questions later but Galen and I were just curious about Hannah Drew's first will. We didn't know if you could tell us or not. Was Margaret a beneficiary under the old one or was the will changed because they met during the play?"

"I don't see why I can't tell you, Mrs. Delaney. Frankly I've wondered if the will was a motivation for her murder."

Elizabeth just responded with one word. "Yes." And hoped he knew she meant - that she wondered too.

"I don't even have to look up the old one. It was very clear and simple. Everything was left unconditionally, without any stipulations, to Lisa Coulter."

"Did Ms. Coulter know about that will?"

"I have no idea. Hannah did not confide in me about that."

"Did she know about the new will?"

"I don't know that either, Mrs. Delaney."

"Do you have any idea why Hannah changed and had a new will written."

"No." He hesitated. "But you might ask those friends of hers from New York."

"Okay, thank you very much, Mr. Andrews. I appreciate you sharing the information with us. Of course we won't tell anyone else."

When she hung up the phone, Elizabeth's mind was working rapidly. And then she got her cell phone and called Galen.

Chapter Fifteen

Galen drove to work Monday morning with a happy heart. They'd gotten together with George and Linda Sunday night to discuss buying the Manor House. The purchase was agreed on with the stipulation that if they decided to move again, or in the event of their death it would be specified in the will, that the Tates and/or their descendents were given first opportunity to buy the house back.

The agreed-on amount included the Guest House, and Galen and Elizabeth had insisted that any time the Tates, Fowlers, or anyone else in the court needed to use it, they were welcome, without charge.

After the business was settled the two couples played several games of "Hands and Feet" a knock off of Canasta, which was one of Galen's favorites. He and Elizabeth played it sometimes but it was more fun with two couples. Now that he wouldn't have to commute in the future, he hoped they could spend more time just having fun. And maybe his daughter and her husband would want to play sometime too.

His daughter - the very thought of Jenny filled his heart with more joy than he had ever imagined having a child could. And then he felt guilty because Bits didn't have one. But really, they were too old to begin with an infant. He shook his head and turned his mind back to the professional move.

***

The meeting went very well. All necessary decisions had been made. The three of them were usually in agreement and today's was only slightly different. The High One reminded them of the Rede "Do what you will, so long as it harms none." And they'd all agreed. Those two had no idea who was responsible for what happened to Hannah Drew, and hopefully never would. But the other one's idea and determination was suspect. Would that harm anyone? The tension was relieved when the High One ended the meeting of the coven by asking, "When shall we three meet again?" And they all laughed.

***

Elizabeth was just putting a chicken in to bake when the front doorbell rang. She was surprised to see Sara by herself, usually the two girls came together.

"Come in, Sara! I'm so glad to see you." She could tell the girl looked nervous but hoped her greeting would bring some ease to whatever was causing the stress.

"Hi, Ms. Delaney. You sure I'm not bothering you?"

"Not at all, I've got about an hour before time to cook the vegetables for supper. And if we're still talking, you can just come in the kitchen and we'll talk while I work."

A smile drove out the nervousness from Sara's face. "Or I could help you. I love to cook."

Elizabeth led her into the parlor and they each found a comfortable seat. "That's neat that you love to cook. Who taught you?"

Sara shrugged her shoulders. "I taught myself. My mother isn't into all that homemaker stuff." She took a deep breath. "And that's why I wanted to talk to you. You're a shrink right?"

Elizabeth couldn't repress a smile at the description of her profession. "Yes, I guess you can say that. I'm the kind of shrink that doesn't give medicine, just talk therapy."

"And you give advice?" The stress showed on the girl's face again.

"Well, I like to think I lead people to make their own wise decisions."

Sara nodded. "That sounds good. That's what I need. To make a wise decision."

Elizabeth waved her hand. "So let's hear it." Then she stopped. "Oh, I didn't think. You just got home from school and must be hungry. Would you like a snack?"

Sara tilted her head. "Maybe after we talk about my decision."

Elizabeth agreed.

"It's, well, this is hard. But ... you know I'm much better and I could go home now. I hate to intrude into Reggie's family. I mean, I love living there; life for me has never been so good. But they are a family and I'm not part of it." She was silent for several seconds. "And I think Reggie is tired of me sharing her room. She doesn't say anything but I think we were better friends when she didn't have to put up with me all the time."

Elizabeth smiled. "I understand. I mean I really do. I was brought up in Catholic boarding school. I lost my family - all of them - when I was eight years old."

The sympathy in Sara's eyes was unmistakable. "I'm sorry."

"I'm sorry to change the subject from your problem. I just wanted you to know that I really understand when you just don't feel like you fit in."

"So, should I leave the Tate's now? I can't stand the thought of going back to my mother's house - and her men. But..."

"Do they ever try to bother you now, Sara? The men, I mean."

"Not any more. That one that I told you about did, but I made him stop and I glare at the others so hard, I guess they're afraid to."

Elizabeth laughed. "Good for you!"

That made Sara laugh too.

Then Elizabeth said "Is there another alternative?"

Sara took a deep breath. "I could go to Social Services and ask to be placed in foster care. If they knew what my home life is like, they would probably already have done that. But, Ms. Delaney, you never know what kind of home those places are either. Some are good but some aren't." She shook her head as if remembering stories she'd heard. "And they might move me out of Simpsonton too. And then I wouldn't see Reggie anymore. Or you!" The girl looked very sad.

Elizabeth looked at her in silence for a moment. "Can we pray?" When Sara had given her consent, Elizabeth continued. "Father, we come hand in hand," she reached over and took Sara's hand, "not just in the flesh, but in the spirit Lord. We are Your children, Your little girls, and we need Your wisdom. Please show us what Sara is to do, where you want her to live, and how soon she should move out of the Tate's home. We ask it in your Son Jesus' Name, in His nature, as your beloved children. Amen."

Sara was beaming at her when Elizabeth opened her eyes.

"Sara, let's go get some snacks. And you know, I think I am going to give you some advice."

"Okay!" The girl sounded jubilant. "What is it?"

"Wait to make your decision until after the wedding next weekend. Give Reggie lots of space. And please come to the wedding and to the brunch we're having here the next day."

Sara nodded. And they headed to the kitchen.

Elizabeth really enjoyed her time with Sara that afternoon. The girl insisted on peeling the potatoes, which was one kitchen chore Elizabeth was not fond of doing. And she showed Sara how to make her own favorite broccoli casserole.

But when she invited the girl to have supper with them, Sara shook her head. "I don't want to intrude."

"You wouldn't be intruding."

"Well, some other time, when we know ahead, okay?"

"Okay." It was sad to see someone so fearful of causing people to want her to leave. Elizabeth had never experienced that. She had been the rebellious one who not only wanted to leave, but had. For fourteen glorious months she had been Grace Love, the teenage evangelist who led many to, and back to, the Lord. Until the authorities found out she was really Elizabeth Miles and took her back to the convent boarding school where some very disapproving nuns took her back - reluctantly. But since she was legally a ward of the Church due to her only surviving relative being a nun, they had no choice.

She hugged Sara good-bye and went back to the kitchen to finish up the remaining chores for supper. There weren't many, thanks to the girl. The cooked broccoli casserole was still in the oven on low, the mashed potatoes, made with real butter and heavy cream the way Galen liked them were in a bowl in the microwave ready to heat again, and the baked chicken was on the table on a platter covered with silver foil.

Elizabeth took a sack of mixed salad from the refrigerator and cut up chunks of tomato, onion, and cucumber to add to it. She smiled as she looked at the clock. The love of her life would be here any minute. And they had some important things to talk about.

Finally she saw him come up on the back porch and smiled at him through the glass windowed door. But he didn't smile back.

"What's wrong, Sweetheart?" She put the salad down and went over to give him a hug.

"The Market Presidency here in Simpsonton. They told me this morning it was mine and then called me in this afternoon and said there could be a problem. Someone here in Simpsonton, a big investor, wants the job."

"Oh no! Oh, Galen." Then she lifted her head up. "Let's pray right now. I know God wants you to have that job."

Her husband smiled. And then looked up toward the ceiling. "Hear that, God? I guess You better get busy."

She playfully hit him on the arm. "I'm serious. Come on. Sit down and let's pray." So he sat at his normal place at the kitchen table and she stood behind him with her hands on his shoulders.

"Dearest Father, I believe with all my heart you want us here, for Jenny, for Galen, for our new friends, for our marriage, and for the Bank too. Galen is so good at his job - well, You know that. But Lord, we do want your will above all. And if I'm wrong, show me. But until and unless you do show me differently..." She waited in silence for a minute. "I am praying against someone else getting that job. Galen will be President of the Simpsonton Bank. I'm saying it in Jesus' Name! So be it."

Galen turned to look at her. "My, you are really, uh, full of yourself today." He held up his hand at her look. "I mean you must be full of Himself, you prayed so confidently."

She smiled. "That's better." And she turned the microwave on and got the homemade bleu cheese dressing out of the refrigerator.

The next morning Elizabeth was relieved when Deputy Collins answered the phone at the Sheriff's office.

"Hi, this is Elizabeth Delaney. I wonder if you could give me some more information?"

"Closin' in on the killer?"

"I hope so but I need some more information."

"If I got it, you got it!"

"I would like to know how to phone Cal Morgan in New York. Would that be okay to find out?"

"Don't see why not. Hold on a minute." She could hear a drawer being opened. "Got it. You want the other guy's number too?"

"No, I don't think so...well maybe in case I can't get in touch with Cal. Yes, please."

When Elizabeth had both Cal Morgan and Albert Shaw's phone numbers written down, she dialed the first one.

"Cal Morgan speaking."

"Hi, Cal. This is Elizabeth Delaney from Simpsonton. I met you during the Wizard of Oz play. I hope I didn't call at a bad time."

"No, ma'am. I'm not busy at all. Excuse me just a second." She heard him call out "Al, would you hand me my coffee cup?"

So they probably were an item and lived together. That meant that together they had a million dollars.

"Okay, I'm back. Has some new information happened? I mean have they found out who killed Hanley yet?"

"No, I'm sorry to say. But I called to find out something, because the attorney doesn't know and thought you might. Do you know why Hannah...Hanley changed her will?"

There was a long silence. Then she heard a sigh.

"I guess so. I mean she's dead now so it doesn't matter if I tell what she told us. We were good friends you know. She was a very nice and kind lady."

"Yes, I know."

"She said not to say anything, but I know you're not a gossip. And she trusted you and your husband a lot."

"Thank you." Elizabeth waited patiently.

"Well, the reason was, she found out that her friend Lisa was into witchcraft."

Elizabeth made her voice stay calm. "Really?"

"Yes, Hanley said that since she was playing the Wicked Witch of the West, Lisa brought up the subject and said she thought Hanley might be interested. Hanley pretended to be just to find out how deeply Lisa was into all that. And she found out that it was pretty deep. Lisa was a part of a convent of witches or something like that."

Elizabeth was glad he couldn't see her smile. "A coven. That's hard to believe in a little southern town like Simpsonton."

"Yes Ma'am. Coven. That's right. Hanley was shocked too. And really disappointed. She told Al and me, she just couldn't leave Lisa all that money to go to witches. And the little girl who played Dorothy was a relative so she took us with her and changed her will."

"How interesting. I'm so glad she had you and Al as friends."

"Yes, she was really sad about Lisa. She was very generous to Al and me too. You know she paid us to come down but she also gave us a lot of money when she made the new will. It wasn't payment to witness it or anything, and she said she wasn't putting us in the will but she wanted to thank us for being such good friends." His voice broke a little. "She really was a good friend to us. I'm going to miss her a lot."

"You were good friends to her too, Cal."

"When you find out who murdered her, will you let us know?"

"Of course I will. I'll call you when we know."

"Thanks. And it's a good thing I won't be there because I'd want to kill whoever killed her."

"I understand. And maybe, when the new theatre opens, the Hannah Drew Theatre, you and Al could come down for the opening."

"We'd be honored. To honor her, you know."

"Yes, I know." When Elizabeth hung the phone up, she found herself thinking about the personality of Hannah Drew. Deeper than she'd thought. But what now?

She wouldn't call Deputy Collins yet, not until she had some more information. But what? Who else was in the coven? Maybe she needed to learn more about witchcraft. She started toward the library and her computer but then hesitated. She'd heard that people could get your information if you went on their online sites. Maybe she'd just go to the public library.

That decided, she locked up and went toward the new parking garage. The company really had done a wonderful job.

When she got to the library, she was surprised to realize how happy she was to see Glenda Taylor. The librarian looked as though she was glad to see her too.

"Hi, Elizabeth. How are you?"

"I'm doing fine. It seems like forever since the play but it hasn't been that long." Then she remembered the lawyer's office. "And of course we were both at the reading of the will. That was a surprise, wasn't it?"

Glenda shook her head. "I still haven't taken it in. It means, well it means a lot." And she blushed.

"You and Brandon will be busy with all the plans for the theatre, building and all that."

Glenda smiled. "Can you keep a secret?"

Elizabeth laughed. "I'm a psychologist. Part of our profession is to keep secrets."

"Brandon and I have other plans too, but we're going to wait a little while before announcing them. We're engaged. To be married, I mean."

"How wonderful!" Elizabeth reached out and hugged the younger woman. Then she realized the implications. "Hanley, I mean Hannah, do you think she realized the situation with you two?"

Glenda laughed. "I think so. Brandon was the only man in the cast or crew who wasn't gazing at her the whole time."

Elizabeth smiled. "I noticed that too. He looked at you all the time. But I thought it was because you were the Director. I see I was wrong." Then she looked at the clock on the wall above Glenda.

"Can you help me? I want to do some research about witchcraft. Are there any books on the subject?"

Glenda gave a slight shudder. "Yes, they haven't been checked out for a while. A couple of years actually. The last time I remember anyone getting them was, strangely enough, Carolyn Brock."

That was definitely not what Elizabeth was expecting. "Carolyn Brock? That is strange. Did she say why?"

"She said somebody had recommended that she read them, that's all." The librarian shrugged her shoulders.

When Elizabeth had the books in hand and checked out in her own name, she asked one more question. "Anybody else check these out?"

Glenda shook her head. "But they could have read them at the study tables in that room. I wouldn't know."

"Okay, thanks." Elizabeth reached over the counter and hugged her newly affianced friend. "And I won't tell anyone your news until it's made public."

Glenda smiled. "Thanks. Hopefully it won't be long. We talked about announcing it at the opening of the Christmas show - which will still have to be at the high school, I guess." She made a face. "Oh, I don't know if it has anything to do with witchcraft, but Carolyn Brock picks up a key to the library every Wednesday at closing time for some kind of meeting she has downstairs. Then she slips it through the book drop after she locks up."

"She never said what kind of meeting?"

"No. I never asked. That's tomorrow night. Should I ask her?"

"No," Elizabeth shook her head. "If it is witchcraft, and I can't imagine her involved in that, it could be dangerous."

"Dangerous? Why?"

Elizabeth couldn't, and didn't want to, share about the witchcraft signs at the murder scene. "Oh I don't know. If she didn't want it to be known, she might, what? Put a curse on you or something?"

They both laughed and said goodbye.

When Elizabeth was in her car, she realized her hands were shaking. But then she remembered, Carolyn Brock was in full view of everybody during the crucial time of the murder.

And she wasn't going to report this yet to Deputy Collins. Not until after tomorrow night.

When Galen walked through the door that night, he looked like a new man. She looked at him with a question in her eyes.

"It's all settled, Bits. The person that wanted the job here at the bank backed out. Evidently it was a woman and her husband objected and called the bank and said she was withdrawing. They asked if she could tell them personally so he put her on, and she did. They wouldn't tell me who it was." He drew her into his arms.

She breathed a sigh of relief. "I'm so glad, Sweetheart. When does it happen?"

"A week and a half. Well, two weeks from yesterday. A week from next Monday. Time to let me get some things completed in Lexington, and for the current President here to wind up and have his staff give him a retirement party."

She held him closer. "I'm so glad. We are very blessed. All our dreams are coming true."

"Most of mine already have." He hugged her even tighter.

Elizabeth already decided not to tell him anything about what she learned about Carolyn Brock or Lisa Coulter and witchcraft. She had something more important - at least to her - to discuss.

She waited until after supper, hamburgers and homemade french fries. She'd spent so much time on the phone and going out to the library that she wanted to fix something quick but something he liked so she stopped by the grocery and got hamburger meat. And this was one of his favorite meals. He'd told her about the hamburgers he loved at a hamburger dump during his school days. The burger was fried with chopped onions and then tomatoes and Miracle Whip were added to the bun. She was responsible for the fries herself, fresh potatoes cooked in Canola oil, soft on the inside but crispy on the outside. It was one of her favorite meals too.

After they'd finished with dinner and dishes, they went to the back porch as usual.

"Wonderful night for September," her husband remarked. "Not too hot and not too cool."

She agreed. And then, "Galen, I want to talk to you about something."

"This sounds serious."

"Yes, it is. Very serious. So, please think it over before you respond."

"Okay Bits." He reached out his hand and took hers. "Is it about having a baby?"

"Well, not exactly but sort of." She laughed nervously. "It's about Sara Conley." And she told him about the visit after school.

"Galen, what if we took her in for the rest of her high school years? She could have the spare bedroom. And she's very quiet and very respectful. And we could tell her we like to be alone in the evenings. And she's used to being by herself so I'm sure that would be okay with her. And she could ride with the Tates when she and Reggie need to go somewhere. Like youth group or play practices or..."

"Whoa!"

Elizabeth looked up at him, startled. Until then she didn't realize she was staring at the floor while she talked. And he must not like the idea or he wouldn't have stopped her.

But when she looked he was smiling. "It's okay, Bits. If that's what you want, it's okay. I've been feeling bad because I have Jenny. Well of course you have her too, but you know what I mean."

She nodded. "Yes, then each of us would have a daughter to share with the other." She moved over to his lap and sat down. "You really mean it?"

He nuzzled her neck. "Yes, I mean it. It would have been great to have our own child together. But we'd be over sixty by the time it graduated from high school."

She nodded. "You're right. But with Jenny and Sara, the relationships and responsibilities are something that we can handle. Without stress, I think."

"Agreed. So did you mention this to Sara?"

"No, of course not. Not until I talked to you. And I think we should talk to her mother first. I don't want to get her hopes up."

"When? Now?"

"Well it's still fairly early. And Sara is at the Tates. She wouldn't know if we went to their apartment."

He gently stood up, sliding her off of his lap. "Let's go."

Chapter Sixteen

Elizabeth knocked on the Tate's door and could tell Linda was surprised to see her.

"Come on in! You usually call first so I didn't expect it to be you."

"I couldn't wait any longer. I have some news." She wouldn't tell Linda that Sara was afraid of being unwanted by Reggie so she skipped over what led up to their decision.

"Galen and I went to see Sara's mother last night."

Linda Tate looked surprised again but didn't say anything.

"I hope you don't mind. But we asked if we could take custody of Sara for the rest of her high school years."

Linda's mouth literally dropped open, "And Galen is okay with this?"

"Definitely." She couldn't tell Linda about Jenny either, not yet. She'd promised them both to keep their secret. "Mrs. Conley agreed. I think she was relieved that we'd be handling all her expenses. But, Linda, is this all right with you? I mean, did you and George want to keep her here?"

Linda laughed. "No. I mean we didn't. It's fine with us. In fact it solves a problem. We couldn't make ourselves turn her away but I think Reggie wants her room back and it will be great to have just our family together again." Then she laughed for the second time. "Though Reggie and Chuck will probably resume the arguments they used to have all the time."

"I'm so glad! Well, not about the arguments. But that it's okay with you."

"And we'll still have Sara here in the court so that will be great. We really do love her."

Elizabeth nodded and gave a sigh of relief.

Then she told Linda what she'd not told Galen about yet - the talk with Cal Morgan, and finding out about Lisa Coulter being involved in witchcraft, that being the reason for the changing of the will. Then she told her what Glenda at the library had said about Carolyn Brock checking out witchcraft books a few years ago.

"Wow. So it's possible that both of them are into Wicca or something like that?"

"I checked out the books on witchcraft myself and read a little this morning." She shrugged and gave Linda a guilty look. "I didn't let Galen know about all this. Anyway, it takes three to make up a coven and the deputy said Lisa was part of one." She laughed. "He called it a 'witch's convent'."

Linda joined her in the laugh. Then looked very serious. "This is yucky."

That's when Elizabeth brought up her main reason for sharing the information. "It seems that Carolyn Brock has a meeting at the library after hours each Wednesday. I wondered if maybe you might go with me and watch to see who shows up."

"Tonight? What time?"

"I have no idea. But I didn't like the thought of going alone. The library closes at five thirty on Wednesdays. Maybe we could drive there around six?"

"Hmm, I do have leftover roast and the vegetables that were cooked around it. So I don't have to cook and guess that would be okay. But what do we tell our husbands and the kids that we're doing?"

"Galen is working late because of the move. Oh, it's a week from next Monday that he'll start here."

"Yes, he called George last night and told him to start the house deal process, that the job was settled."

Elizabeth smiled. "Well, we could say we were going to Walmart. And we could go after we find out who attends the meeting. That way we wouldn't be lying."

"You're good, Elizabeth." And Linda grinned.

They parked a few blocks away from the library on the dot of six. The bell from the library rang the time. The building used to be a church and the little town was used to hearing the bell, so the city kept it up when they bought the building. Elizabeth and Linda walked as nonchalantly as possible along the sidewalk across from the library. And then they walked past it a few blocks. When they walked back and passed it again, they saw the back of a car turning into the parking lot at the back of the library. It was Carolyn Brock's Rolls Royce.

As far as they could tell, she hadn't seen them so they breathed a sigh of relief.

"I have an idea," said Linda. "Let's go over to the street behind the library. There are a lot of trees behind the parking lot. We could go in there and see who else comes."

"Ah, now you're the one that's good!" Elizabeth smiled at her friend. When they walked around the block and were settled in the grove of trees and bushes, they looked at their watches and it was nearly six thirty.

"Look," Linda whispered. Sure enough, Lisa Coulter drove up in her much less fancy car and parked beside Carolyn Brock's.

"That's two. There's at least one more." Elizabeth whispered back.

And as she finished speaking, a figure walked down the drive to the parking lot and joined Lisa as they went to the basement door.

Elizabeth and Linda looked at each other in shock.

"I didn't expect that," Elizabeth said. The third member of the coven was Ron Lockland.

They waited until the bell rang seven o'clock, decided there were no more members of the coven coming, and left for Elizabeth's car.

When they were settled in, Linda asked, "What do you think? Was one of them the murderer?"

"Well," Elizabeth said, as she started the car, "Carolyn Brock and Ron Lockland have unshakable alibis. So if it was one of the three, it has to be Lisa Coulter."

"But why?" Linda asked.

"Money, the reason most crimes are committed."

"Yes, but is a million dollars worth killing your best friend? Hannah Drew was like a sister to her."

Then Elizabeth explained. "I don't think Lisa knew about the new will. She thought she was going to inherit somewhere between fifty or sixty million dollars."

"Wow. That IS a lot of money."

"When the attorney read that she would inherit a million dollars, she gasped. Did you notice?" When Linda nodded, she continued. "I thought at the time it was surprise at getting that much money but now I think it was surprise at getting that little money."

When they pulled into the Walmart parking lot, Linda said, "Now what are we going to shop for?"

"I haven't got a clue," Elizabeth answered. "Wait a minute. Yes I have. What does Sara need in the way of clothes?"

"Practically everything. I've been meaning to take her somewhere. But we were all so busy and she got hurt. And... I know, you could give her a gift card."

"That's a pretty lame excuse for being gone to Walmart for over an hour."

Linda laughed. "You're right. Let's shop for something. When are you going to tell her?"

"Tonight when Galen gets home if it's okay with you."

"Yes, that's fine. Oh, look! It's Tinker Bell pajamas. She loves Disney movies and especially Peter Pan for some reason."

"Great! I'll get the pajamas and give her a gift card with it so she can pick out her own things."

***

When Galen got home, Elizabeth greeted him with the news that she'd talked to Linda about Sara moving in with them.

"Would it be all right with you to call Sara to come over now and ask if it's okay with her?"

He was very tired but he smiled gently and hugged her. "Call her now." Then he looked at his watch. "It's just eight thirty. Kids are up much later than that these days."

Shortly the doorbell rang and Elizabeth ushered Sara into the library where he had settled himself in his favorite recliner. He smiled warmly at the teenager.

"Glad to see you, Sara. Everything going okay?"

"Yes, Sir. And are you okay?"

He nodded. "Well, sit down, we want to talk to you about something."

Elizabeth took her hand, led her to the leather couch, and then sat down beside her. Galen nodded for her to start the conversation.

"Sara, I didn't tell anyone else except my husband about your visit yesterday."

The girl nodded and said in a whisper, "Thank you."

"And then we did something else. We didn't tell her about it either, but we went and talked to your mother last night."

Sara's eyes widened but she didn't say anything.

"If you want to," Elizabeth looked deeply in Sara's eyes, "only if you want to, your mother said you could move in with us."

Sara removed her hand from Elizabeth's and put it over her heart. "Really?" She looked over at him. "Really, you'd want me?"

He smiled at her. "Yes, we'd want you. Would you want to come?"

She looked back at Elizabeth and then threw herself into his wife's arms. And burst into tears. Elizabeth smiled at him and he could see the tears in her own eyes.

"Yes," Elizabeth said. "We want you very much."

Sara kept sobbing for a few minutes and then sat up straight. "I can't believe it. I thought the Tates were the nicest people in the world but you..."

He spoke up. "We're no nicer than the Tates. We just need a child in our home. They've already got two and we can't let them be selfish now, can we?" He grinned and Sara smiled back at him.

"How long? How long can I stay?"

"Well, at least until you graduate from high school. Then we'll see what God wants for you." He hesitated and then added. "Why don't we all pray now?"

They all three stood up and held hands while he led them in prayer. "Father, thank you that you are going to share this daughter of yours with us. Help us to be good substitute parents to her, and guide us in all we do, and the decisions that are made for her future."

Elizabeth interrupted. "And Father, please help Sara to be happy here in Tapestry Court."

Sara added, "Thank You, God, for the best present ever, besides Jesus dying for me."

When they'd all said, "Amen," Elizabeth added. "Oh, nobody but the Tates know this yet, but we're buying this house and going to stay here. Galen is going to be the President of the local bank here in Simpsonton."

Sara beamed. "God is so good."

Elizabeth said, "Oh, I forgot. I have a welcome to the family gift for you." She brought out a wrapped package.

Galen noticed Sara's hands were shaking as she tore off the paper and opened the box to pull out some pajamas and a gift card. Then she gasped. "For me?"

"Yes," Elizabeth said softly. "I heard you like Tinker Bell, and I'm sure you'd like to pick out some other things for yourself."

"Will you take me and help me pick them out?"

"I don't know anything about kid's clothes these days."

"Please, Mrs. Delaney!" The girl looked pleadingly into Elizabeth's eyes.

"Okay. But you know, we need to find something else for you to call us instead of Mr. and Mrs. Delaney."

"But what?"

Galen spoke up. "What about Aunt E and Uncle G?"

Sara laughed. "I love it." Then she turned to Elizabeth. "Is that okay with you?"

Elizabeth nodded. "And I think we'll not announce this until Saturday morning at the brunch, if that is okay with you. And you can move in that afternoon."

Sara hugged Elizabeth first and then turned to him. "You don't know, you just don't know. I never knew my father or had any uncles, and..." She turned back to Elizabeth. "You know what my mother is like. I think she has some sisters but they don't speak to her so I never had an aunt either. Aunt E and Uncle G. I really love it."

"Group Hug" said Elizabeth. And they all obeyed.

After Sara had left, Galen suggested they tell one person about Sara moving in.

Elizabeth grinned and agreed. They walked over to Jenny's house since they could see the lights still on in the living room and the couple were obviously glad to see them. After Galen had hugged his daughter and shaken hands with Joel, he and Elizabeth sat down on the couch.

Joel was the first to ask why they were there. "Is this just a spur of the minute visit or is there something you want to talk about?"

Galen laughed. "Both. It's spur of the minute but we want to tell you something." He looked over at Jenny. "How do you feel about having a sister?"

She looked shocked. "You have another daughter somewhere?"

Elizabeth glared at him. "No, Jenny."

"Sorry. I didn't realize how that would sound. You are my only daughter and I love you very much. But we thought you should know that we are taking in Sara Conley for the rest of her high school years. Her mother is an alcoholic who has men in their home all the time. She doesn't need to be there."

"Oh, I'm glad... Daddy." The 'daddy' came out a little stilted but his heart was happy that she said it. "I've met Sara several times and she really seems like a nice girl."

Elizabeth said, "She is. This was my idea. We missed your teen years so this is like a gift to us." She and Jenny exchanged warm smiles. "She's going to call us Aunt E and Uncle G."

Jenny and Joel both laughed and Joel nodded and said, "That's good!"

Jenny added, "So now we'll have a family of five for Thanksgiving and Christmas and all that."

Galen nodded. "Oh, we aren't going to tell anyone else about this until the brunch Saturday. We'll announce about Sara staying with us, and then we'll tell the big news, the best news I've ever had to tell," He looked over at Elizabeth, "right up there with the news that your stepmother loves me and married me."

"Thank you, Daddy." This time the 'Daddy' came out naturally.

***

When they got home, Elizabeth said "We need to talk." And she sat down on the couch in the library.

Galen looked are her doubtfully but sat down next to her instead of going to his favorite chair. "What's wrong, Bits?"

She sighed. "I'm afraid you are going to be upset with me but I just had to find out."

"Find out what?"

"I called Cal Morgan and he told me why Hannah Drew changed her will. She found out that Lisa was into witchcraft, in a coven. And there were definite signs of witchcraft at the murder scene according to Deputy Collins."

"Well, Bits, that's not upsetting to me. And if you've reported all this to the Deputy, what's the problem?"

She grimaced. "Well...I haven't told him all that. And there's one more thing."

He held out his hand. "And?"

"I found out that Carolyn Brock holds an afterhours meeting at the library each Wednesday night."

"And?"

"And so Linda and I went by there tonight on our way to Walmart and there were three people who came to the library. They were Carolyn, Lisa, and Ron Lockland."

Galen's eyebrows went up. "From what you've told me, I can't imagine Ron Lockland hurting Hanley Drew. He was in love with her."

"And, Galen, he and Carolyn both have an alibi for the time of the murder. That leaves only Lisa Coulter."

"I thought they were best friends."

"But Lisa thought she was going to inherit everything. That must be why she gasped when she found out she was only going to inherit one million."

"So, you've told all this to the Sheriff?"

"No. Not yet. I wish we could find something to prove she did it."

He looked at her sternly. "Elizabeth, you are not going to put yourself in danger, understand?" Then he smiled. "You've got two daughters now to take care of yourself for. And me!"

She smiled and nodded. "I know." Then she stood up. "Want some hot chocolate?"

"Sounds great. And I'm glad you see that you have to stay safe."

She nodded again. There was no way she could tell him what she planned to do.

The first thing after Galen left for work Thursday morning, she called Deputy Collins with her idea. He wasn't thrilled with it but finally agreed. He said he would be bringing someone else with him though.

"That's fine. As long as you trust them and don't tell them before tonight exactly what is going on."

"Done. But, Ms. Delaney, what time and where will we meet?"

"I'd like to take both cars, yours and mine. I'll just go to the house and you can be there too."

"Ma'am, we got to meet to get you hooked up."

"Hooked up?"

"Yes, to one of them recorders. We got 'em here. You just put your key on it - it looks like a key chain. And then everything that's said will be on it."

"But will you be able to hear what's going on?"

"Yes Ma'am, the kind we got sends out the sound when it happens. And we got the thing that hears it. We'll be right there to come in when she confesses."

She breathed a sigh of relief. "Well, I can come and get it anytime today. She's in school and wouldn't see me there at the office."

"Uh, would it be okay if I brought it to you there at the Court?"

"Of course, if you'd rather."

"Yes'm. I'd rather."

Elizabeth was so glad that Galen was working late and the Tate family, along with Sara, were having dinner with the Fowlers. Their son and his family flew in that afternoon and Linda drove Harold and Lucy to pick up Lydia, and greet their son and his family when the plane came in, even though the family were going to rent a car to drive back to Simpsonton.

So there was nobody to wonder where she was or what she was doing.

On the way to Lisa Coulter's house in Bayberry Subdivision, Elizabeth found herself dreading the encounter. But it had to be done. There was no other way. And she was the only one who could do it.

She checked her watch to make sure that Deputy Collins would be arriving in the neighborhood at the time they agreed on. It was just right. She drove into the driveway, pulled the key from the lock and let herself out of the car.

When Lisa Coulter opened the door at her response to the doorbell, she didn't look happy to see Elizabeth.

"May I come in?" Elizabeth didn't smile or pretend it was a friendly visit.

Lisa shrugged. "I guess so."

She didn't offer Elizabeth a seat so they both stood in the entrance hallway. "What do you want?"

"I wanted to tell you that you need to turn yourself into the police."

The teacher snorted and said, "Sure. What on earth for?"

"For the murder of Hannah Drew, the murder of the girl that was with Sara the next night, hurting Sara and trying to poison her. Is that enough?"

When she mentioned the poison, Lisa's head flew up. Obviously she wasn't expecting that.

She was silent for a minute before she responded. "I don't know what you're talking about."

"I think you do. You see, I saw you slip behind backstage and go to Hannah's dressing room."

"You're lying!"

Of course Elizabeth knew that was the truth, but she stood her ground. "I just didn't know at the time what motive you could possibly have, so I thought it couldn't be you who murdered her."

The other woman was at a loss for words for several seconds. Then she snorted again. "Ridiculous. Why would I kill Hannah?"

"Money."

"No, I didn't kill her. And what do you mean about those girls? I had nothing to do with any of that either."

"Yes, you did. Sara remembered later what the car looked like that hit them outside the movies. A black PT cruiser, your car."

"Ridiculous. And why are you here? Why not the police. Haven't you told them all your stupid ideas."

"No, I haven't." She wasn't lying; she hadn't told the police, only the sheriff's deputy. "I wanted to give you the chance to turn yourself in."

"Well, that's interesting." Lisa reached down and opened a drawer of the hall table. The next thing Elizabeth knew, a gun was pointed at her.

"I'm so glad you haven't been to the police. Because now they will never know."

Elizabeth kept her face from looking the way her insides were feeling. "You can't kill me with that gun - what about my car in your driveway?"

"It won't be in the drive. You and I are going for a ride in it and you and your car will be found somewhere else, both out of commission. Permanently."

Elizabeth felt a chill of fear go through her whole body. Surely it was time for Deputy Collins to come. But what if he wasn't here yet? Was Lisa going to kill her here and would she be already be dead when they took their drive? She stalled for time.

"I certainly underestimated you, Miss Coulter. I thought you would be glad that I gave you the chance to confess instead of turning you in."

"You stupid b..." She never got the sentence finished because the front door burst open and Deputy Collins and a man in a city police uniform burst in.

"That's enough," the policeman said. "Put that gun down."

"She was trying to rob me, Officer." Lisa Coulter's face was suddenly frightened looking. "I was just trying to protect myself."

Deputy Collins spoke up as he pulled his own pistol out. "Put that gun down. We heard everything that was said."

The frightened looking face turned to rage as she turned to Elizabeth. "You lied to me. You said you didn't tell the police."

"I didn't." Elizabeth looked her in the face. "I told the deputy, that's the sheriff's department, not the police." She looked at the policeman. "And I didn't know he told the police."

Lisa looked at her gun and then at Elizabeth, as if she wanted to have one last murder on her list of accomplishments.

Elizabeth realized she was holding her breath.

But then the other woman's shoulders drooped and she laid the gun down on the table.

Deputy Collins patted Elizabeth on the shoulder as the police officer picked up the gun and read Lisa Coulter her rights.

Collins motioned for her to go outside with him. "You want to gimme that key chain now, Ms. Delaney?"

She nodded, and took her key off the device. "Thank you, Deputy."

"You want me to drive ya home now? I don't mind. I ken get a ride home from the Court. Call a friend or somethin'."

"No, I'll be all right."

"If'n yer sure."

"I'm sure." And she smiled at him.

As soon as she got home and saw that Galen's car was still not in the garage, she walked to the Tates.

Chuck answered the door. "Hi, Mis D. We just got home. I got cousins, Erik is just my age and Brad is two years younger. It was fun."

"I'm so glad, Chuck. I forgot about the dinner but I'm really glad you had fun."

"You okay, Mis D? You look kind of funny."

"Well, I feel kind of funny. But I promised you that you'd be the first to know. Is it okay if I tell your family about it at the same time."

"You mean about the murder?"

"Yes."

He looked disappointed but said, "Sure."

She took pity on him and said, "I'll tell the whole story to them all, but here's the name." And she whispered Lisa Coulter's name in his ear.

He did a thumbs up. "Never did like her. Come on. And tell us everything."

Linda greeted her with obvious surprise again and at Elizabeth's request, called the girls downstairs and George from the living room.

When they were all seated around the kitchen table, Elizabeth told them all the details, leaving out Chuck's part in the investigation, because of her promise.

"You can tell." He said to her. So she did - about him seeing the figure in the court that night, and finding the witchcraft symbol in their shrubbery.

His mother gave him one of 'those looks.' But didn't say anything.

"So, by now she is in the county detention center. And with all the charges, I doubt the Judge will trust her out on bail."

Reggie spoke up. "That's a relief." She looked at Sara. "Now it won't be so uncomfortable going to school."

Sara spoke quietly. "I forgive her."

They all stared at the girl.

"Thank you, Sara." Elizabeth said softly. "We all needed that reminder." She looked at George.

He nodded. "Let's pray." And held out his hands. When
all of them were holding hands around the table, he led
them. "Thank you, Lord, for Sara's safety and great compassion. Thank you that Hannah Drew's murderer was
found and arrested. We hold her up and ask you to come
into her life and drive out her need for involvement with
witchcraft. Amen. Wait, we also hold up Mrs. Brock and
Ron Lockland. Please set them free too. Thank you. In Jesus' Name, Amen."

Elizabeth was already in bed when Galen came home.
At the sight of him she burst into tears. He sat on the bed
and held her close while she confessed through heaving
sobs.

When she calmed down, he drew back and looked at
her.

"Bits, we need to make a change in our marriage. I was
dishonest with you about my past. But you've been dishonest with me about your future, what you plan to do.
We both need to be completely open with each other."

She nodded and pulled him back to herself.

Chapter Seventeen

The red roses sat displayed in the bedroom of the Guest House and because of Hattie everything was spotless. All was in order. And Galen would be home early today in time for the wedding. She hoped the couple would enjoy their ceremony as much as she and Galen had loved theirs. Harold Fowler would be performing it, as he did theirs. It must be a real joy for him and Lucy to see Lydia Tapestry not only mentally and emotionally healed and healthy but in love and being loved. It was something they never thought would happen after her years in care facilities.

The sun was shining and the temperature was in the seventies. A perfect day, not too hot and not too cool. Elizabeth called Linda. "I'm going to run up to the Archer's store and pick up some things to have for breakfast in the Guest House in case Lydia and Stephen don't want to come for the brunch. Is there anything you need?"

"No, but I'd love to walk with you."

The two women met on the sidewalk. Linda said "We have a lot of work to do this afternoon since the wedding is at five."

"I know. That's why I wanted to get this out of the way first. How many will there be for the wedding?"

Linda smiled. "Not as many as for yours. The Archers won't even need to clear out their parking lot. We've got, besides the wedding couple, Harold and Lucy, you and Galen, my bunch - all five of us, one of which will be yours after tomorrow." She grinned and went on counting. "Jenny and Joel, Charles and Mindy, Hattie, and Bill. Oh, and I invited the Archers if they want to come but I'm not sure if they'll close the store that early or not. And Jackson Fowler and his family So either nineteen or twenty-one . And we've got plenty of food to cover whatever. Oh, Elizabeth, you'll really like Jackson and Cindy Fowler. They're a lot of fun. Turns out he's pretty famous in his own state, has a huge church. That's why they don't come in very often."

"Yes, and I know Harold and Lucy miss being with them." She paused while Linda opened the gate at the front of the court, and reflected that was the gate through which she first entered Tapestry Court. "You know, I think we should talk to Jackson and Cindy about it and if it's okay, your family and mine could fly Harold and Lucy out there for Christmas, as a gift."

"Yes! That's a wonderful idea."

After they had picked up some bagels and cream cheese, added cereal and milk, and found out the Archers were closing at 4:30 so they could come to the wedding, Elizabeth and Linda headed back to the court.

"I know it's none of my business, but did you tell Galen about last night?"

"Yes, and he told me I needed to be truthful with him upfront from now on." She didn't mention his own dishonesty about his past. But that would come out tomorrow. She was surprised at how difficult it was not to tell Linda.

But she said, "Linda, thank you for being you. I've never had a best friend before."

Linda smiled and though neither of them could hug because of the full sacks of groceries, the looks in their eyes made up for it. "I had one once in high school but she disapproved of my decision to marry George instead of going to college and she dropped me. So you are my first real best friend."

Elizabeth felt her heart hurting for her friend. "I didn't know. And I'm sorry that happened to you. I'll never drop you, ever."

"I know." And they walked in silence back to their houses.

The wedding was beautiful. It took place on the sidewalk of Tapestry Court where Elizabeth and Galen's wedding had been. Stephen Richardson rented a beautiful archway of white wrought iron and that was where the vows took place. He had on a black suit and Lydia was dressed in a beautiful white dress that came to her calves. It wasn't a wedding dress but it was perfect for her and for the occasion.

Linda had been right about Jackson and Cindy Fowler. They were a lot of fun. Jackson insisted on giving the toast with the fake champagne. "To my Aunt Lydia and new Uncle Stephen. May you have a perfect life and marriage. And may you always glorify our Lord Jesus Christ." Then he took a sip of his drink, as did all the guests, and proceeded to pour some of the beverage on his own head. When he turned to his wife, she backed away. "No, not this time, Cutie!" And they all laughed.

Chuck tugged at Elizabeth's sleeve. "Can I show Erik and Brad the secret garden?"

"Of course. Did you want to show them anything in the house too?"

"Nah, you gave me the ships and I already showed them those."

She smiled. "Okay." She was so glad that she gave the collection of ships to Chuck on her own wedding day. After all they had belonged to his grandfather.

The next morning Elizabeth got up early in order to crack open the eggs and prepare them for last minute scrambling. When she had them in the refrigerator, she fried sausage, both pork and turkey, and put them in silver foil. Everyone was coming at nine and nearly everything had to be done at the last minute, fried hash browns, biscuits, gravy made from mixes she bought at the store. She also had cantaloupe to cut up and grapes to wash.

By nine they had all arrived, everyone from the wedding except the Archers, all the Tapestry Court family - that's what it felt like - a family, and the four extra Fowlers.

All the breakfast dishes were put on the counter in the kitchen and some were seated at the table there, some outside on the back patio, and some at the table in the library. Elizabeth didn't know when she'd gotten so many compliments on her cooking.

And then when the food was gone, Galen went around and asked if everyone would join him outside. The morning was warm and everyone would be able to be either on the patio or the lawn behind it. The newlyweds were seated at the table, glowing and holding hands. Harold and Lucy were there beside them as were George and Linda. The rest gathered round, except that Galen motioned for Sara and Jenny to join him and Elizabeth right outside the back door.

"We have some news to share and wanted to do it now before Jackson and his family need to leave"- he looked at his watch-in fifteen minutes."

He looked over at Elizabeth who put her arm around Sara. She announced, "First we want to tell you that Sara will be moving permanently to Tapestry Court." She saw a look of shock in Reggie's eyes and hurried on. "She is coming to live with Galen and me."

Reggie's expression turned to joy and she was the first one to start clapping.

Then Elizabeth turned to Galen and held out her hand, telling him to continue their announcements.

He grinned and pulled Jenny Anderson to his side. "You all knew that Jenny was adopted but what you didn't know, nor did we until my wonderful wife discovered it,"- and he smiled at Elizabeth- "was that Jenny is my biological daughter. Her mother died at birth and I never knew what happened to my child. Us coming to Tapestry Court and finding you all as friends and family was wonderful enough but to find my daughter after all these years, and hearing her call me Daddy, is also a God thing." Jenny wiped away tears and leaned in closer to Galen.

Elizabeth said, "So now you know that we have two daughters, both here in Tapestry Court!"

Everyone applauded again. And then it was time to say good bye to the younger Fowler family.

When the dishes were all washed and put away and they'd stood at the front door and waved goodbye to the rest of the court, Galen pulled Elizabeth to himself. "How long do we have before our youngest child moves in?"

"She said she'd be here around supper time. She and Reggie wanted to talk and had some games to play."

"Good." He said, "Time alone." And he led her back into the house.

Monday morning Galen went back to Lexington for his final week at work there. Elizabeth hugged him goodbye and then hugged Sara goodbye as she started down to meet Reggie for a ride to school.

What a weekend. For that matter what a three months! Murder, witchcraft, wedding, daughters. The phone rang and interrupted her musings.

"Mrs. Delaney?"

"Yes."

"This is Ron Lockland, from the Wizard play."

"Yes, Ron. I know who you are." She was surprised but made her voice sound friendly.

"They told me you are a psychologist, a counselor, is that right?"

"Yes, I am."

"I wondered if I could make an appointment to talk to you."

She hesitated. Could this be a ploy to get even with her for Lisa's arrest? Does he even know about it all? Has he seen Lisa?

"I don't have an office anymore, Ron."

"But I'll meet you anyplace, at a restaurant, anywhere. I really need some help."

Her heart melted. Of course he did. "Tell you what. Would you mind meeting here at the court, at Reverend Harold Fowler's house? He has an office and I'm pretty sure he'd let us use it."

"Yes, Ma'am. I mean no, I wouldn't mind. When? Anytime you say."

"Let me call you back in a few minutes after I ask him."

After she explained the situation to Harold Fowler, he agreed that for her safety it would be best. And he would be right outside his door, which was the house nearest the front gate, when she let Ron Lockland in. And he'd be right outside the door to his office while they talked.

They agreed on two that afternoon.

When Elizabeth and Ron were settled in Harold Fowler's office, after declining coffee from Lucy, the man put his head down on the desk.

"Ma'am, Mrs. Delaney, I've been so stupid."

She could barely hear him but didn't say anything. She also heard some sniffles and realized he was crying.

He lifted his head, wiped away the tears, and continued. "I was in love with Hannah Drew from the time we were children. She was kind to me but never interested in me that way. To tell the truth I don't think she had a romantic bone in her body. I thought she was in love with that Cal guy but then it turned out she wasn't. I guess she just wanted me to know there was no chance for me." He sighed.

"I'm sorry, Ron. That must have been really painful for you all these years."

He nodded. "I felt so helpless and so worthless. And I guess that's what got me into the mess."

Elizabeth's heart began beating harder. Was he going to confess?

"This is hard to admit but I guess I needed something to make me feel important so I let Lisa talk me into..." He stopped. "You know that Lisa is the one who killed Hannah?"

She nodded. So he didn't know about her part in Lisa's arrest.

"Well, she talked me into joining a witchcraft thing she and Mrs. Brock were into. They had to have one more person for it to be legal or something. And they let me be the one in charge. I guess it made me feel important. But I never did really buy into it. I think they did though. It was a power thing. Lisa was trying to have power over the education system in our town and Mrs. Brock wanted power over the financial system. They said I could be the one in power over the entertainment." He shrugged. "But that didn't work out. Brandon and Glenda are over that. And Mrs. Brock didn't get appointed to be President of the bank when the other guy retires."

Aha! That was the woman who wanted Galen's position. She nodded. "And Lisa can't do anything about the education system now."

"Yes, Ma'am. That's right. And I feel stupid and guilty. Why did I go along with all that stuff? And I really had no idea that Lisa killed... my Hannah." Tears came to his eyes again. "I just couldn't believe it when she called me from the jail. She wants me to be a witness for her good character or something. But I can't, Mrs. Delaney. I just can't. The whole thing, including the part I played in her coven just makes me sick."

"I can understand, Ron. You know, when people feel rejected and unimportant, others can con them in to things they really don't want to do, just so they can feel included."

His eyes widened. "Then you do understand?"

"Yes, I do. And I think you will come out of this and find a good life, the life God planned for you. You said you didn't buy into the witchcraft thing but what do you believe about God?"

"I think He's disgusted with me. I was raised in the church and I believe Jesus died for everybody, so that would include me. But I've always put other things before him."

Elizabeth reached out and took his hand. "God is not disgusted with you, Ron. I promise. He loves you and is so glad you are seeing things clearly now. He wants you to talk to Him the way you've talked to me. Would you mind if we called Reverend Fowler in to pray for you and with you?"

He shook his head. "No, Ma'am."

After Elizabeth had relinquished her spot behind the desk to Harold Fowler and taken the chair beside Ron, she explained the situation, which she knew was really unnecessary because Harold had been listening, but she didn't want Ron to know that.

Within twenty minutes, Ron Lockland had confessed, received forgiveness, and felt the love of God enfold him.

Harold ended with a prayer. "Lord thank you for this young man. I know you have a wonderful plan for his life, one that will help others. Oh, and Lord, would you send him the wife you have in mind and prepared for him. And prepare him to be a good husband. In Jesus' Name, Amen."

After Ron had been let out the front gate by both of them, Elizabeth turned to Harold. "You sounded pretty sure there is a wife out there for him, when you were praying."

He nodded. "I just pray as it comes to me. A few months ago, I found myself praying for Reggie's safety, when I was only asked to pray for her audition. It surprised me, but I prayed it."

"Yes, I'm so glad you did."

***

Elizabeth had another surprise that day. It was around five and Sara was in her new room doing homework when there was a buzz from the garage.

"Miz Delaney, it's Deputy Collins. Can I come in jest for a minute?"

"Of course, Deputy." And she pushed the button to open the gate.

She met him at the front door and he stepped into the hallway.

"I won't stay. Just wanted to bring you your half." And he grinned as he handed her two one hundred dollar bills and a fifty.

Did you miss the first installment in the Tapestry Court series?

It's been ten years, but is the murderer still living in Tapestry Court?

Christian psychologist Elizabeth Daily flees to the gated community of Tapestry Court for a sabbatical to untangle parts of her own life, both professional and romantic. But the shadows of decades-old secrets interwoven with present day mysteries there are distracting - and may be dangerous. Among the old world setting and charming neighbors, does a decade old murderer hide behind a tapestry of lies? And can Elizabeth discover the truth in time?

Books by Amy Barkman

To Love Again

Everyday Spiritual Warfare

Which Witch?

Kentucky Adventures

You've Got to be Killing (e-book short story)

The Patsy Patrol (e-book short story)

A Kiss is Still a Kiss (story in collection)

Tapestry Court Series

Murder at Tapestry Court

Danger at Tapestry Court